PARADISE BEVERAGE BAR

BENJAMIN CRAWFORD

Contents

1

CHAPTER 1

The streets were commonly packed during the day with the daily bustle of action. The cabmen with their horses and traps could barely drive through the streets as pedestrians were spilling off the sidewalks.

Tobias pushed and dodged through the crowds when someone seized him by the shoulder causing his heart to leap out of his chest.

He hurled around with a full fist but suddenly refrained from punching the face he came to recognize.

"Ben! You scared the life out of me!" Tobias exclaimed. "My apologies," Ben said. "You're reaction was quite aggressive though." "I was in deep thought," Tobias said as he and his friend walked side by side.

"Anyway, what are you doing out here?"

"I was heading to Blue Jay's Pastries for bread. Where are you headed to?" "Ted's Butcher to purchase meat for Brutus."

Tobias went with Ben to the bakery and Ben in return went with his friend to the butcher. "Can I get an order of a pound of beef?" Tobias asked. He walked into the butcher shop that smelled of blood and meat. "Grounded or whole?" Ted Wilson asked. Mr. Wilson, more so known as Mr. Butcher due to his aggressive and intimidating attitude, looked at Tobias with a pair of fierce black eyes shadowed by tufted brows.

"Whole," Tobias answered. Tobias leaned over to Ben and put his lips to his ear. "I wonder what's his problem. He's seems to be unhappy constantly."

"What's my problem?" Mr. Butcher suddenly turned around with a long meat blade in his hand. "What problem do you have with others' business and their lives? Where is your respect?"

Mr. Butcher threw a bag of meat to Tobias and took his payment. "Get out of my shop!" he raised his voice aggressively. "And mind your own business!"

Tobias hurried away from the butcher's shop with his friend at his heels. "He's fortunate that no one in Pristine Hills has the option of purchasing meat elsewhere" Tobias said. "I agree" Ben said.

When Tobias made it home, he got in the kitchen with an excited Saint Bernard by his legs to chop up the beef into pieces. He then served Brutus a portion of the red meat in his stainless steel bowl before freezing the rest. "That dog won't be the only thing you will care for for the rest of your life, Toby," Tobias's mother walked in the kitchen. His mother, Anne James, was a woman in her late thirties.

"There will come a day when you will marry and have a family to care for."

"I don't have to think about that right now," Tobias said who was twenty-one years old. "I'm still in collage and have many years ahead before I earn my master's degree for a lawyer. I don't even have a job or property of my own for a family." "You do have property," Anne said. "What?" Tobias started in confusion.

"Come with me."

Tobias followed his mother to her's and his father's bedroom. She opened her wooden closet and started digging through her clothes to get to the back.

"You are the heir of gold, my dear," she said, turning around with a long yellow envelope made of a rough material. Mother and son sat on the edge of the bed.

"And this whole house. This paper here is a will I signed before you were born. This will says that this house which is mines and the remainder of gold that I own will be yours after I am gone." "Mom, you haven't made it clear yet as to where did you get this gold from or how is this house yours," Tobias said irritably. "How come this major fact was concealed from me for twenty-one years."

"I didn't want you to know of this too quickly," Anne said. "I intended that you know when you were older and mature to understand reality.

This gold I inherited from my mother. I used half of it to buy this house, the mare Sienna, the trap, and the furniture.

The remainder of the gold I locked away in a safe located behind my closet. The key so you know is buried in the dirt of my flower vase. You're father doesn't own anything. He was a poor man when I met him. You're poor father worked as a construction man. He helped build this house however but I'm the one who bought it so it's mines.

Now Toby, this property is yours and so is the gold. What you have in your hands is what people dream of having. If any scandal or robbery occurs when you inherit this property, you have this will and three witnesses who witnessed me sign it. Your father, the maid Clara Ambrose, and my lawyer Ethan Paige.

You must protect this will with your life.

There is people out there who will if they find the will, steal and destroy it. Then they will rob you or create a scandal to make it look like the property isn't yours.

But you have witnesses and you mustn't let this will go. Do you understand me?"

"Yes I do," Tobias said nervously for the way his mother was speaking had him thinking that she feared a robbery or scandal in the future. "But I don't understand why you are so scared. Do you have a reason to believe that something terrible as you say will happen?"

"No, my Toby," Anne said calmly placing her hand on his leg. "If I had a reason to believe something terrible would happen, I would have warned you now so that you take precautions. The only reason I fear this greatly is because my mother experienced a robbery when I was young. There was an evil-hearted servant in the house who stole her will to me. Fortunately before he could create a scandal, the police recovered it."

"Does father know where the gold and the key is?" Tobias asked. "I never told anyone," his mother said. "Even Clara and she's my closest friend. There's no reason for them knowing. It's not theirs. You cannot tell anyone about this, Tobias. This is your secret and if you spill it to the wrong people, that will mean no good for you." "I promise I won't tell anyone, mom," Tobias said. "I'm a grown man. I'm not some excited child who heard they are getting a favorite toy and now they spread the news to their friends. When will I get it though?"

"When you graduate from college and when my time is up in this world," Anne said. "That's when you will start a life of your own and you will need it."

2

CHAPTER 2

S aturdays and Mondays were the best days of the week for Tobias. Studying government and laws as was required to become a lawyer was difficult and sometimes overwhelming for him. So when those precious days of rest and freedom arrived, Tobias made sure to take full advantage of them.

Today happened to be Monday, June 1, 1800. Tobias arranged his black vest and neatened his dark hair with a comb. He grabbed his black jacket which extended to his knees and slipped it on.

He left his bedroom and walked into the living room where Brutus greeted him excitedly. "I'll be out for a bit, Brutus," he told his dog. "You be a good boy. I don't want to hear that you tore apart a shoe or broke a vase with your tail." Tobias ruffled the dog's fur and played with his ears which he absolutely loved.

"Where are you going, young man?" came the voice of Tobias's father, Bennett James. "I might go to the juice bar," Tobias said putting his hat on. "I'm going to hang out with Ben." "Today's his day off?"

"Yes, he has Monday and Tuesday. Let me get going. Bye dad." Tobias met up with his friend Ben Hudson.

They greeted each other with a handshake and a 'how are you?' "Do you any idea of where you want to go?" Ben asked. "Maybe to the juice bar. They make good juices and smoothies there." "Sounds good to me."

Tobias flagged down a hansom from the street and ordered the driver to take them to Paradise Beverage Bar. When they arrived, Tobias gave the driver his rightful fee and then he and Ben walked into the bar.

"I'll pay for the drinks," Ben said. "Since you paid for the cab." "You wouldn't have a choice" Tobias said.

Ben laughed and nudged his friend in the arm.

They ordered two glasses of fruit punch and took their drinks to a table in the corner. "How's college coming along?" Tobias asked. "It's coming along fine. I enjoy medical and I'm eager to become a doctor, but even the things you enjoy become difficult and irritating at times" Ben explained.

"Sometimes when I think of how many years I have until I earn my master's degree, I feel like quitting because I don't have the patience to wait for all those years," Tobias said. "There's times when I think about just becoming a cabman or something like that." "That sounds like laziness. I see it this way. It's worth years of studying to become something big and important than to not study and end up riding around in a hansom or trap for hours on end."

"Cabmen are important just like doctors and lawyers," Tobias said. "Without them we wouldn't be at this bar right now because I wasn't going to walk."

"Yes they are important but who wants a job like that."

"If no one wanted a job like that then there would be no cabmen." "Please, Toby," Ben said. "Those cabmen didn't want that job. They didn't have no choice. The majority of people don't have money for school and college. It's a blessing if you come from a family who has the money for education and cares about you becoming someone big. Be grateful, Toby, and take college seriously. You don't know what will happen tomorrow that will enable you from attending college and achieving your dreams."

Tobias didn't get to say something in response when the people in the bar were suddenly aroused by something outside. Tobias and Ben pushed there way to the entrance of the bar. "Police?" Ben said. "What happened? Why are they rushing?"

"Maybe a robbery" Tobias said lowly as he stared after the black horses and official carriages riding by at full speed. Suddenly, one carriage came to a halt.

A man descended the carriage and came walking in Tobias's direction.

The man had a professional air about his attire and appearance. He was somewhere in his forties with a solid serious face and a hard dark eyes that pierced out from beneath tufted brows.

The man wore a hat, a long coat, and a suit beneath.

He ascended the steps projecting from the front of the bar, and stopped when he was two steps apart from Tobias. "My name is Detective Dwight Greyson," he said. "I'm a detective from the DPA. Something terrible has occurred and I believe you should be there."

The first thought that came to Tobias's mind was that someone robbed his gold. "Did someone rob my house?" Tobias asked. "See for yourself, young man" said Mr. Greyson. Tobias exchanged an nervous glance with Ben.

However, he went along with Mr. Greyson and off they rode down the street. Tobias noticed a scene ahead after driving for five minutes. People were crowded around something between an alleyway that appeared to be the center of attention.

The policemen whipped their horses to a stop and they jumped off the hansoms in a hurry. "Away from the crime scene!" an experienced inspector called out in a loud voice.

Tobias and Mr. Greyson descended the carriage. Tobias's father came in a hurry over to him. "What happened, dad?" Tobias asked nervously. "Something terrible has happened, son," his father said. Tobias noticed tears threatening to spill from his father's eyes.

"Where's mom?" he asked.

When his father didn't have the strength to say it, Tobias was thrown into a state of panic.

He rushed to the alleyway and froze in his steps when he saw before his own eyes the body of his poor mother. She lay on her back and the whole chest area of her light pink dress was stained in crimson blood.

Tobias's mind was racing like an engine out of control. He couldn't think properly, he didn't know what to do, and he felt like this was all a dream. Suddenly, he hurled around at the crowd of spectators. "Get away from my mother!" he yelled. Rage and pain bursted through his voice. "She is not a show nor entertainment for you guys watch! I don't want to see those pathetic looks of sympathy on your faces! Get out of here or I'll rip those looks off for all of you!"

Never in Tobias's life had he spoken so harshly anyone. He would have never done so if he were in his right mind. He walked up to his mother's body, kneeled down, and scooped her upper body into his arms. "Mom," he said in a trembling voice. Tears were already spilling from the sides of his eyes . "Don't leave me. I need you."

When he realized she wasn't returning, he broke into a painful sob and buried his head under hers. "Don't leave me," he cried. "Don't leave me. I can't without you. I need you!"

3

— • —

CHAPTER 3

"Tobias! Are you there?" a distant voice called his name. His head was fuzzy but his senses were returning slowly. Tobias's eyelids rose, fell, and then rose again. He blinked several times to clear his vision.

He found himself home and with his concerned father by his side. "What happened?" Tobias asked in weak voice. "You fainted away from shock," his father said. "The police interrogated me and they want to do the same with you. Are you ready?" Tobias just nodded his head slowly. His father rose. "Mr. Greyson will come in a moment with Detective Jason Emery. Miss Ambrose, bring him a glass of water." "Yes sir" the maid said.

Tobias's father stepped out of the house where the police were and Miss Ambrose came with a glass of water. "Everything will be fine" she said setting the glass on the table. "Nothing will fine!" Tobias suddenly shouted and threw the glass on the floor.

His father rushed in with Detective Greyson and Emery.

"Tobias, what is this?" he asked. "Nothing will be fine!" Tobias shouted again. "How can this woman tell me it will be fine? I just lost my mother. That means losing my life, my purpose, and half of me!I don't anyone coming in my face with a sympathetic look and telling me that everything will fine!I want that killer found and given their own medicine.Or else I will find them and give me a piece of the real me."

Tobias left everyone frozen and speechless before he disappeared down the hallway. A door slammed and everything went silent. Tobias was greeted by his dog who had been sleeping on his bed.

There came a knock to the door. "Tobias, Mr. Greyson must come in to question you" Bennett said from outside. Tobias wiped his face with a handkerchief and then Mr. Greyson came in his room. He turned the desk chair around to face Tobias and seated himself on it. "I'm sorry about your mother," he said. "I promise I will do everything in my capability to find her killer. Now there are some questions I'd like to ask you. I'll try to make this short. How often did your mother go to work?"

"Three times a week," Tobias replied. "Monday, Tuesday, and Wednesday." "Did she have friends in the neighborhood?" "She was a quiet woman who stood to herself and didn't make acquaintance of others. But her only best friend that I know was Clara Ambrose, the maid. She did make acquaintance of Dolores Armando."

"Do you know how and why?" "When Dolores moved into Pristine Hills like some three years ago, she didn't know the area. So my mother helped her get by and from there they became acquaintance but never friends."

"What was the relationship like between your parents? Had there been recent arguments or debates?"

"My parents were always a peaceful and loving couple who seldomly argued. I can't even remember the last time they got into." "Did your mother have recent or past rivals?"

"Her rival is Wendy Hudson. Wendy has a son by the name Ben and he's actually my friend. But our mothers were the opposite. I heard that before my mother, my father was going to marry Wendy. But when he changed his mind and married my mother, Wendy blamed my mother for her miserable state of life. Her parents forced her to marry this man, John Hudson, who is currently her husband. I know she hated him in the beginning. For the next few years, she despised my mother. When she would see her on the same road or shop, she would shoot her a nasty look. However she grew out of that childish behavior. Ben and I spoke a lot about the subject because it had to do with our mothers.

He told me like some five years ago that his mother actually came to love her husband after all those years of hatred. He said that he overheard her saying to him that she was sorry about the hatred and that she didn't care for my father anymore. Ever since they have been getting along well."

"Do you know the reason for your father changing his mind?" "He came to love the kind of woman my mother was. He always spoke highly of her. She was beautiful, well mannered, and educated."

"Is there anything of interest that you could tell me of your mother's past?" "All I know is that she came from a rich and educated family. I know once that there was an attempted robbery on her mother's gold. Some evil-hearted butler in the house was the culprit."

"Did your mother inherit any gold?" "Yes, she did. Yesterday she told me of it for the first time." "Who knows of the gold?" "My father, Miss Ambrose, and my mother's lawyer Ethan Paige."

"Does anyone know where was it hidden?" "No, only I. My mother said it wasn't anyone's business to know where it was because it's not like they are getting a portion." "Do you know the name of that butler who attempted the robbery?" "No."

"That's all I will ask for now. If I think of any questions I need to be answered, I will call for you. Thank you for your patience."

Based on the information that Detective Greyson and the police collected from Tobias and Bennett, they sent for Wendy Hudson and Dolores Armando. Wendy Hudson was a thin and pale nervous woman in her late thirties. Her clothing showed of a simple fashion. She wore a light colored dress, gloves, and a hat with a simple bow over her brown bob. With her was her son Ben Hudson.

Ben Hudson looked more like his father than his nervous mother. His young face was hard and set and his dark eyes shone with confidence. His fashion was simple like that of his mother's. A simple brown suit with a hat and that was it.

Dolores Armando was the opposite of Wendy. She was a graceful and confident Hispanic woman in her early thirties. She wore over her elegant figure a blue dress, gloves, and black bonnet over her black hair which was in an elegant bun. Her tan face was decorated with a light touch of makeup. The women and young man waited in a hallway for Detective Greyson to call them for interrogation. It wasn't long before he exited a room and said, "Mrs. Hudson, you may come now."

Wendy walked into the room where she found Detective Emery sitting by a desk. She sat in the opposite chair and looked at the detective with a nervous pair of dark eyes.

4

Chapter 4

"Why are you nervous?" Detective Emery asked, leaning his arms on the desk. "I know why the police suspect me," Wendy said. "I just want to make it clear that my hatred against Mrs. James faded away five years when I came to love my husband. I'm happy now and I don't care for Mr. James. Even if I was still holding that grudge, it would never lead me to commit murder. I'm not that woman."

"We know Mrs. Hudson," Mr. Emery said. "But the police don't solve cases like this. We wait, observe, and collect suspicious behavior, facts, and hints. Anyway, I will ask you questions and you will give me an honest answer. Where were you at two pm today?"

Wendy swallowed nervously and took a moment before speaking. "I was home preparing lunch" she answered. "I heard that you came to love your husband five years ago. How did that happen? Did it happen magically?"

"No, I let myself let it happen," Wendy said. "My son was fifteen years old at the time. I had been holding that grudge against Mrs. James for fifteen years. But I came to realize that being upset didn't do me any benefit. I was just a miserable woman. I knew inside that John was a good man.

Even though he knew that I didn't love him, he didn't force me to and he was always kind to me. It was as if he knew some day I would come to love him. When I freed that anger from my spirit and let my heart open up to the fact that I had an amazing husband, I was finally able to love him and accept that Mr. James wasn't for me and I didn't care anymore."

"Sounds like you went through a spiritual battle of fate and acceptance," Detective Emery said. "Do you know why Mr. James changed his mind and when did he?"

"It was two days before my wedding. Mrs. James moved into the neighborhood a week before my wedding. She was a rich woman and wanted to build her dream house in Pristine Hills. She hired construction workers from the company and one of them was Mr. James.

His boss put him in charge of the project and so he and Mrs. James were interacting quite often. Two days before my wedding he told me that he had something to confess. He told me that Mrs. James asked to marry him and that he accepted it. I asked why didn't he reject the proposal.

He explained that Mrs. James was more like the woman he wanted to marry and build a family with. Anyone would choose Mrs. James over me. She knew how to cook, she was educated and well mannered, and she was a very hygienic as well as beautiful woman. Not to say that I'm dirty or don't know how to cook, but I've always been a rather hyper girl who didn't enjoy the ordinary woman's life."

"That's all I have for you for now. If I think of any other questions I'd like to ask, I will send a letter for you. Thank you for your patience, madam."

"You're welcome." Wendy rose from her seat and walked over to the door. "What's your perspective on me? Suspicious or innocent?" she suddenly asked. Detective Emery looked at her and so did Detective Greyson who had been standing by the door. "We will decide as the case develops," he said. "Mr. Greyson, it's Ben's turn."

$$5$$

Chapter 5

Ben entered the gloomy interrogation room with Detective Greyson behind him. Ben took his seat, the door was shut, and Greyson took his post by it. "Take off your hat" Emery said. Ben did as he was told. The light penetrating through the barred window shone directly on his face giving the detective an advantage to study his facial expression.

"I question and you answer with honesty. No lies or tricks or you will be exposed sooner or later and when that happens you will regret it." "I regret nothing" Ben said. "Where were you at two pm?" Mr. Emery asked.

"At the Paradise Beverage Bar with Tobias."

"His claim is true," Detective Greyson said. "I saw him when I pulled over to pick up Tobias."

"When did you return home?" "At around two-twenty after Tobias went with the detective." "Was your mother home?" "No." "Do you know where she was?""The maid told me she went grocery shopping at two pm." Detective Emery and Greyson looked at each other.

The same thought came to their minds. She lied.

"When did she return?" "I don't know exactly when but it was probably twenty minutes after I got home."

"Did she have groceries with her?" "It was just a few vegetables. The maid asked her why did she take forty minutes just to buy vegetables. She said that she got caught up with a friend." "Did your mother really come to love your father five years ago?"

"Yes she did." "Bring Mrs. Hudson back in."

Detective Greyson left the room and returned with a very nervous Wendy. "Yes sir" she said trembling like a scared rat. "I shall ask you again. Where were you at two pm?"

"I already answered that question." Detective Emery rose from his seat and walked over to Wendy. "You didn't answer it with honesty. You're son here just told me that when he arrived home, the maid told him you were out shopping. You left at two pm and took forty minutes just to buy a couple of vegetables.

"I don't know what you are talking about" Wendy said and hurled around for the door knob. But Detective Greyson blocked it off instantly and Emery grabbed her by the arms. "Why are you fleeing from the truth?" he asked roughly. "Are you guilty about some-thing?"

"I'm guilty of nothing" Wendy said, pulling away from Emery's grasp. "Then why did you lie?"

"What would you do if you were in my shoes? If you were a top suspect and you knew that your chances of being charged with the murder were high. What would you do?" "I would be honest because being caught by the police in lies is far worse than saying the honest plain truth even if it sounds suspicious. You and your son can go but know that you are being watched." Wendy glared at the detective before leaving with her son.

6

CHAPTER 6

"Next" Emery said. Greyson exited the room and returned with Dolores Armando. Dolores sat on the chair and stared at Emery with confidence written all over her face. "Take off your bonnet."

She did so and placed it on the table.

"Ask me anything you like" she said in her Spanish accent. "Just know that whatever you say here will be used against you in court," Detective Emery said. "I'm aware but I'm not afraid" Dolores said. "Where were you at two pm?" "I was hanging laundry out of my window and I saw Mrs. James exiting the building infront of mines." "What did you do?"

"I called her out as any acquaintance would and only got to ask how was she before she was shot right infront of my eyes." "Did you see the killer?"

"Why would a killer commit murder while exposing their identity?"

"What did you do when she was shot?" "She froze when she felt the bullet go through her heart. I asked what was wrong until I saw blood spreading on her chest and then she fell. I rushed for the police and ran down to her." "How often did you guys meet?"

"Not very often but we did have tea or coffee during the evenings." "Besides Mrs. James, do you have any other acquaintance or friends?"

"Wendy Hudson is my friend." "The whole Pristine Hills knows of the expeditions that your husband embarks on. He leaves every six months and returns three weeks later. Do you have any idea what he's doing during that time?"

"He told me that he visits his sickly mother and other relations." "Do you know to where he travels to and is this new?" "I asked him where does he travel to but he said that I wasn't allowed to ask that. Before our marriage he told me about these journeys and said that I wasn't allowed to interfere in his family business. He told me that if I wasn't satisfied I didn't have to marry him. He seemed truthful to me though.""When did Samuel leave?" "Yesterday night."

"How long have you and Wendy been friends?"

"I met her on the second year of being in Pristine Hills. We have been friends for two years."

"Did she ever speak to you about her dislike against Mrs. James?" "No, she didn't."

"That makes sense because she said she recovered from her hatred five years ago and you moved into Pristine Hills three years ago, which means she let go of her grudge two years before you came. That's all I have for you in the meantime. If I think of any other questions I'd like to ask you, I'll send a letter for you. You're free to go, ma'am."

7

CHAPTER 7

Tobias had his reasons for suspicious feelings against Mr. Butcher/Ted Wilson. The man with his large and muscular intimidating figure and short-bearded cold face seemed to hate Tobias. But he hated everyone in the neighborhood. Tobias felt he didn't mean good to anyone. The way he glared at people who did nothing to him. And the way he would threaten people who upset him by slamming his meat blade into a piece of meat. Tobias thought the man had murderous intentions.

So after the reading the interrogations in the Pristine Magazine over breakfast, Tobias dressed and slipped a fake mustache in his pocket. He then left the house but not before ruffling up Brutus's fur.

Once he was away from the house and on the way to Ted's Butcher, he slipped on the mustache. After a ten minute walk he arrived at the butcher and entered it.

"How can I help you?" asked the man there.

"Where's Mr. Wilson?" Tobias asked putting on a different voice. "He's off from work today" the man said. "Really? Which days does he have off?"

"Monday, Tuesday, and Wednesday."

"So you were working here yesterday?"

"Yes."

"Can I have your name?"

"Who are you?"

"Name's Henry Fisher. I'm a detective from the DPA."

(Detective and Police Agencies)

Tobias pulled out a fake identity card he made last night in preparation for his private and illegal investigation.

The man nodded approvingly. "My name is Steve Wilford." "Thank you for your patience, sir" Tobias said and started for Mr. Butcher's house. He knocked at the door and waited nervously for an answer.

He heard heavy footsteps marching toward the door and then it flung open. There stood the broad muscular figure of Mr. Butcher.

He was in a dressing gown, t-shirt, and pajama pants. "You disturbed my nap. It better be important" Mr. Butcher said. Tobias swallowed nervously but attempted to conceal his fear.

"My name is Henry Fisher and I'm a detective from the DPA. I've been sent to do a couple of investigations around the neighborhood and you're one of them."

"Show me your card." Tobias did so and Mr. Butcher looked at him approvingly. "If you and the police think I'm associated with the murder, then you all have thought wrong," he said. "I don't slaughter people. I slaughter animals."

"We know sir," Tobias said. "But it's not me who decided to interrogate you. It's the police. Where you at two pm yesterday?" Tobias decided to start with the question that Mr. Emery started every interrogation with. "I was working at the butcher" Mr. Butcher answered. "Really? That's interesting," Tobias said. "I happen to know you days off are Monday, Tuesday, and Wednesday."

Mr. Butcher didn't express any signs of nervousness like Wendy did when she was caught in a lie.

"And who did you learn that from?" "Your coworker."

"What is my coworker's name?"

Clever thinking Tobias thought. "Steve Wilford."

Mr. Butcher growled angrily, grabbed Tobias by his collar, and ripped his mustache off.

"Ow, my mustache." "You're not no Henry Fisher. You're that rat Tobias James who buys meat for his little doggy every week." Mr. Butcher threw Tobias against the path of pebbles that projected from his front door. Tobias groaned and tried to get up, but Mr. Butcher kicked him over.

Tobias suddenly jumped up like a tiger and threw a punch into Mr. Butcher's face.

"You liar! Where were you yesterday at two?" Tobias raised his voice angrily. "Were you the one who killed my mother?" Mr. Butcher seized Tobias by his arms and threw him again to the ground. He kicked him over on his face and placed his foot on his back.

"Who do you think you are to challenge me?" Mr. Butcher asked with a growl. "Who?"

"I don't care who I am," Tobias said. "It's not like you can do anything. What are you gonna bring that meat blade to my neck?"

"Leave him!" came a familiar voice. Mr. Butcher removed his foot from Tobias's back and stepped away. Tobias rose slowly from the ground. He stumbled forward before regaining his balance.

"Mr. Greyson?" he said, seeing that his savior was Dwight Greyson. "What's the fighting about here?" Mr. Greyson asked. "This rat came to my door in the disguise of a detective by the name Henry Fisher and started asking me questions."

Mr. Greyson looked to Tobias who appeared beat up. The side of his face was cut slightly by the pebbles and blood trickled down. "He lied about where he was yesterday at the time of my mother's murder," Tobias said. "He said he was working at the butcher but I learned from his coworker that his days off are Monday, Tuesday, and Wednesday. He wasn't working yesterday. He was off and who knows what he was doing."

Mr. Greyson then looked at Mr. Butcher with a startled expression. "You're the second person to lie about where they were yesterday. You guys are starting to make me and soon the police when I inform them think that you all are planned this murder together."

"I was afraid that I would be a hot suspect," Mr. Butcher said. "Considering my past." "You're past doesn't give you an excuse to lie. I will be informing the police about this and they will deal with you. You thought lying would keep your profile clear, but unfortunately it just darkened it like it did to Mrs. Hudson. Come on, Tobias."

When Mr. Greyson and Tobias left Mr. Butcher's house to sit on a bench, Mr. Greyson said, "what in the universe were you thinking Tobias? You're so fortunate that it wasn't Mr. Emery or someone else from the force to have caught you. Do you know how much trouble you could be in with the police? It's illegal for unofficial individuals to perform secret investigations."

"I want to find my mother's killer and give them a piece of my nasty side" Tobias said. "I understand, Tobias," Mr. Greyson said. "But you cannot do it. Let the police do it. I promised you from the beginning that I would find the killer." Tobias looked down at the pavement in a thoughtful manner. "I will let it go."

After biding farewell with Mr. Greyson, Tobias went on his to the woods that lie on the East of the neighborhood Pristine Hills.

He kneeled down by the stream and scooped water into his palms to clean his face and the dried blood.

Once his face was clean, he stood by the stream and stared into the water.

He felt at the moment he could cry out a stream of tears that would never end. Every part of him ached at the thought of no longer having his mother. Goosebumps ran along his arms as the image of his mother's dead body in his arms flashed before him. Tears ran from his eyes down his cheeks and fell into the stream.

Tobias looked at his watch and took it off.

He turned it around to see the message engraved in the back. I love you to moon and back ~ Mom.

The watch he received for his eighteenth birthday and still had it until the age of twenty-one.

Tobias's hands were shaking and his eyes were red and blurry from tears.

His hands suddenly gave way due to weakness and the watch fell in the stream. "No!" Tobias yelled.

He stood up and started running after the watch.

He attempted twice to grab it without getting wet, but he had no choice but to get in the stream. So when he determined that he was close enough to catch, Tobias jumped into the water and snatched the watch.

He got out with the watch tight in his hand.

While attempting his breath, suddenly unfamiliar voices split the silence of the woods.

8

CHAPTER 8

Tobias listened intently to what the strangers spoke about while peeking his head around the trunk. A man with a mustache and glasses handed a chunk of money over to the man with a short black beard.

"Do you think you will be willing do one more job for me?" Mr. Mustache asked. "Only one more job," Mr. Beard said. "I can't risk being caught but I do need the money."

"That's great. I will send you a letter when I need you again" said the other. The men were about to depart when Tobias jumped out from the tree. "Stop there!" Tobias said loudly. The men jumped in scare and froze at the sight of Tobias. "Who are you guys? Are you two the killers of Anne James?"

With one look at one another, the men took off. Tobias started after them. He ran faster than he had ever ran in his life. The wind was screaming in his ears, the forest floor was a blur of passing green, and he felt as if his feet weren't even touching the ground.

So focused was he on his targets that while they saw a log ahead, he didn't and tripped over it. Tobias went flying and then slammed face-down on the forest floor.

Tobias groaned and raised his face which was covered in dirt to see the strangers disappearing in the distance.

"I swear by my flesh and bones that I will catch you and give you what you deserve!" Tobias yelled.

When the strangers disappeared, his face fell to the dirt. His body ached and his lungs were burning from the pursuit. He brought his watch to his eyes and said, "I promise to avenge you, mom."

Tobias laid there for nearly ten minutes letting his body regain its breath and strength. He staggered back to his feet and started retracing the pursuit. He remembered that Mr. Beard's scarf flew off. Tobias found it lying on the forest floor and picked it up.

When he came to the front door of his house and knocked at it, Miss Ambrose opened it for him.

"Oh my, what happened to you?" she asked. "Look at the dirt on your face and jacket." "It's nothing. I just tripped in the woods."

That evening Tobias showered and changed to new clothes. He bandaged the cut on the side of his face and then plopped down in bed. "What a day," he said.

Those seconds of silence were broken by the excited pants of Brutus. "Hi boy. I know I missed you to."

Brutus was all over him and licking his face.

"Stop that, Brutus. That's nasty. Eww. I just washed my face."

"Toby?" the voice of Bennett interrupted the moment. "You're back early from work," Tobias said sitting up and wiping his face with a handkerchief. "How was work?" "It was quite slow," Bennett said. "So I just decided to call it a day. Where were you today?"

"I went to the woods. It's where I've been going since my mother ...you know."

"Why do you have a bandage on your face?" "Tripped over a stone." "Really?" "Yeah, what?" "Nothing. Anyway, get all the rest you need. You will be returning to collage in a week. I'm giving you this week to mourn but I'm still working to provide for you. Plus, you need to fill your time. Work is a way to distract the mind from grief."

The following morning during a breakfast of boiled eggs and toast, Bennett told his son, "Toby, I don't want you going to those woods often."

"Why?" "That's where kidnappers set up their traps. It's quiet, secluded, and free of people."

"Dad, I'm twenty-one. Please tell me who is going to kidnap a brown man."

"You're still very young," Bennett said. "Kids, teenagers, and young adults are the ones who get kidnapped the most. Don't act slow, Toby. You're mother and I taught you enough about this kind of stuff for you to know that you shouldn't be in secluded areas like that. Just stay away from the woods. I lost your mother, I don't need to lose you. Where are you going today?"

"I don't have any ideas," Tobias said. "I'll probably stay home."

When Bennett left for work after breakfast, Tobias waited an hour before heading out in the direction of Mr. Greyson's house. Dwight Greyson was not only a detective but a rich man. His family was considered the richest in the neighborhood. He was a smart man who didn't just depend on his earnings from being a detective.

He saved his money and opened up a diner that went by the title 'The Comfort Zone.' He had family members working there while he did his job. It was known that after years of saving, he bought a duplex house with an estate around it, two horses and traps, and then married his wife Dona Greyson.

As Tobias neared the house it seemed to rise to from the ground. It's details and structure became clearer.

The main section as well as both stalls for the horses were made of sturdy wood. The house was coated in a layer of white paint whereas the points like the attic, pillars, and window sills were in mahogany.

On either of the porch that projected from the front door were well tended bushes from which roses sprung forth. Tobias took the grey brick slab which split through the grassy estate. He stepped up to the porch and knocked at the door.

The door flung open and there stood a blond young lady. The young lady froze at the sight of Tobias and then her cheeks flushed in embarrassment. "I thought it was Father," she said embarrassingly. "He's supposed to be home soon." "How long do you think? I've come to see him" Tobias said.

"You can wait inside. He shouldn't be long." Tobias did a quick sweep of the young lady from head to toe. Her honey blond hair was in a low braided bun with free strands to the front. She wore a sky blue, feathery evening dress that went beautifully with her hair and large green eyes. The lady took Tobias to the living room and left him there to tell her mother of the visitor.

Tobias took a study of the living room and learned that Mr. Greyson had a bright taste in furniture. The cream colored sofas and splashes of green from the plants in the corner seemed to lighten Tobias's spirit. The sofas seemed to add a splash of light to the red carpet and curtain. The light mantel piece matched the light colored woodwork. Two vases of flowers sat on either with picture frames resting in the middle.

The crystal chandelier above gave a sparkle to the living room.

The young lady returned with her mother who looked a lot like her but in her late thirties. Tobias rose from his seat. "My name is Tobias James," he said. "I've come to speak with Mr. Greyson." "I'm Dona Greyson the mother of Natasha here," the mother said. "Dwight will be here soon. Are you the son of Anne James?"

"That's right." "I'm so sorry about your mother," Mrs. Greyson said. "If we could help you in any way, don't hesitate." "Thank you, madam," Tobias said. "I really appreciate it." "Tea or coffee?"

"Coffee please. Milk and one sugar."

"Oh, that should be your father," Mrs. Greyson said at hearing a knock. "Make our guest the coffee, darling."

"Yes mother" Natasha said. Mrs. Greyson returned to the living room with her husband.

"Hi Tobias," Mr. Greyson said, taking off his jacket and hanging it on the coat hanger. "I heard that you wanted to speak with me." "Yes I did. About something very important."

"Dona, will you excuse us?" "Of course."

"Talk to me."

"Yesterday after we departed I went to the woods," Tobias started. "It's where I normally go when I'm going through a lot or just need a piece of mind from people. I was walking to my favorite spot when I heard unfamiliar voices. So I climbed this hill and behind it were two men whom I've never seen before.

One wore a mustache and round spectacles whilst the other had a short black beard and scarf.

Mr. Mustache as I named him gave Mr. Beard a chunk of money. He then asked him if he would be willing to do one more job for him. Mr. Beard said he couldn't risk being caught but that he would be willing to do one more job being that he needs the money. Mr.

Mustache said he would send a letter when it's time to meet again. They were about to depart but I jumped from where I hid behind a tree and told them to stop.

They took off running and I pursued after them. Mr. Beard's scarf dropped during the pursuit and when I los them I got his scarf. I was thinking about letting my dog smell the scarf and then putting him on their trail to see where it leads to. It may or may not lead to something but nothing must be left unturned."

Mr. Greyson looked very grave after hearing Tobias's story. "We can't ignore these strangers," he said after a long thoughtful silence. "Mr. Mustache has obviously paid Mr. Beard for a job he performed. Why did this happen the day after your mother's murder? That can't be a coincidence. And why are these men holding their meetings in such a secluded area? That means they are afraid of being caught just like Mr. Beard said. They have to be the killers. I need to inform the force now."

"What about my idea?" "It's not use, Tobias," Mr. Greyson said, slipping on his jacket. "It won't lead you to nothing. The men obviously didn't stay in the woods. They had to leave and take a trap the rest of the way. I need you to come with me."

Natasha walked in the living room with a cup of coffee and plate of cookies."He doesn't have time to drink it, sweetheart," Mr. Greyson told his daughter. "We are heading out."

"Alright" Natasha said. "Let me get one of those cookies" Tobias said. He took one from the plate and ate it quickly before following Mr. Greyson out of the living room. "Who made those?" he suddenly stopped to ask Natasha. "Me" Natasha said.

"You're a good baker," Tobias said. "Mind if I stop by for more." "Sure" Natasha said and smiled.

Tobias was pulled away by Mr. Greyson who seized his arm.

9

CHAPTER 9

Detective Greyson flagged down a hansom from the road and ordered the driver to take them to the DPA Department. It was a thirty minute ride before the hansom pulled up at the building. Tobias and Mr. Greyson took three flights of stairs to get to the director's office.

On their way to his office, Detective Jason Emery spotted them. "Hey Mr. Greyson," he came up beside him. "What are you doing here with Tobias?"

"You'll learn soon" Mr. Greyson said. They knocked at the director's door and were let in. Frank Dewey the director of the DPA was an elderly man who's hair and mustache was white. He was tall in height and thin in body. Despite his elderly appearance, there was a professional and masterly air surrounding the chief.

"How can help you gentlemen?" Mr. Dewey asked, looking up from his papers. The men each took a seat. "Tobias here has witnessed something that I think you should take into great consideration," Mr. Greyson said. "He will tell you from his own lips."

"Go ahead" Mr. Dewey said. Tobias laid out his story from beginning to end like he did to Mr. Greyson. But he left out the part where he departed from Mr. Greyson because that would give away that he was secretly investigating the case. "And here is his scarf."

Mr. Dewey leaned forward and took the scarf. "I don't think this scarf will be of use but your story is indeed very important" he said. "Are we seriously going to take a story like that from some college student?" Mr. Emery suddenly spoke up. "He could be over-exaggerating. He could've seen the wrong thing. He could've mistaken whoever those men were for being suspicious people."

"Where did he get the scarf from then?" Mr. Dewey asked. "Perhaps it was his father's."

"I've never seen my father own a scarf like this."

"Anyway, you can believe his story Mr. Dewey but I don't. I'm an experienced detective who's been in the force longer than Mr. Greyson and I don't take stories or evidence from college students. As a matter of a fact I had an experience with a college student when I was younger."

"We already know, Mr. Emery," Mr. Dewey said. "The story was never forgotten how a college student killed a rival student, told you a fake story he witnessed, and threw you off the right scent until the last moment."

"Do you know how embarrassing and humiliating that was for me? I shall never believe another story from another student again." "Whatever you say, Mr. Emery. Now Tobias can you draw me a picture of both men's faces?" "Yes sir." "Good. Here's your paper and pencil."

Tobias completely lost track of how long he was outside. After making a sketching of the men's faces, he returned to Mr. Greyson's house with permission to have a coffee and those cookies he loved from Natasha.

He and Natasha exchanged conversation for a while till the sky begun to grow dark. Tobias learned from their conversation that Natasha was a nineteen-year-old student in college who was studying to become a nurse. Beside that, she loved baking, tending to the rose bushes, dressing up, and drawing whatever was before her eyes.

Tobias was impressed by some of the drawings she showed him. They were detailed, colorful, and spectacular. What was unique about each and every one of them was that they had a story behind them.

One drawing showed a sunflower which was the first plant she nurtured by herself. Another showed a little Pomeranian dog that was hers as a child but died due to illness when she was fifteen. Along with drawing and baking she loved riding their horses. But Natasha didn't love everything in the world. She disliked people who mistreated animals and she also disliked those who were ungrateful.

Tobias returned home when the lamps were lit outside.

"Where were you Tobias?" Bennett asked. "I was so worried about you I was about to call the police now. I thought you went to the woods again and someone kidnapped you." "I'm sorry, dad," Tobias said. "I lost track of the time as I was hanging out with Ben." "Really? You do know that Ben isn't off from college as you are for now. So he doesn't have the whole day to hang out. Where were you?" Tobias turned around abruptly as he was walking to his bedroom and yelled, "that's none of your business!"

Bennett froze and so did Brutus who was jumping around Tobias with much joy. "Where I go and what I do is none of your business," Tobias said more calmly. "I'm twenty-one. I'm a grown man who's independent and knows what he's doing. Mom didn't harass me the way you do."

"I'm scared for your safety, Toby," Bennett said. "Did you forget that your poor mother was killed? I don't know who killed her and for what reason. But I don't feel safe and I worry throughout my day and during work about you."

A silent moment overtook father and son as well as Brutus who sat between them staring up at Tobias. "I'm sorry," Tobias said. "I didn't mean to come out like that. It's just...I can't take it all anymore. I miss her and I feel like I can't do move on with life without her."

"I feel the same, Toby. Every morning when I know I need to get out of bed to work I just feel like staying in bed for the rest of the day. For the rest of my life as a matter of a fact. You're mother was everything to me— Bennett paused as grief stung his heart causing tears to blur his vision.

Tobias embraced his father in a warm hug. "She was everything to me, Toby." Bennett sobbed as he said it. Tobias swallowed the lump in his throat and shut his eyes as tears threatened to spill. "I love you, dad." "I love you more."

10

CHAPTER 10

Paradise Beverage Bar was a hot spot during summertime when the heat was unbearable and all that was needed was a cold drink to cool down. Stewart Gibson the owner of the bar ran up and down behind the wooden counter making sure his customers were happy and satisfied.He didn't have many employees save two even though he had the money to hire more, because he was saving for his retirement.

Despite his short and chubby self he moved around like a scurrying rat. When Tobias walked into the bar, he found that his favorite table in the corner was empty. He hurried over to the counter to place to his order.

"There's my favorite customer," Mr. Gibson said walking up to the counter. "How's life treating you?"

"Fine," Tobias replied. "What about you?" "Fine as well. Just doin my job here and save up slowly for my retirement. I'm sorry about your mother." "It's okay. As much I don't like it, it was suppose to happen. I wasn't going to escape it and neither was she. Anyway, do you plan on leaving this place for somewhere else?"

"I plan to stay here. I have my house, my wife, and my children here. Plus, I'm not getting rid of this bar. I'll be hiring two more employees when I retire. But I do plan on traveling the world with my wife. I'd like to spend the rest of my days as an old man seeing the world and what is has to offer. Perhaps I'll go to some tropical island and bring back bizarre fruit for the bar." "You dream big Mr. Gibson but that's a good thing," Tobias said. "Can I get a mango smoothie?"

"Sure thing." Tobias took his mango smoothie to his table and sipped at it slowly while observing everyone else.

The bar was quite crowded but it was spacious and had many tables for everyone as well as stools by the counter.

Couples, friends, and families ordered beverages and sat down to talk and laugh with one another. Tobias felt an ache hit his heart like a hammer. He remembered coming to the bar with his mother every week. Anne's favorite was the strawberry smoothie. They would always take the table in the corner which Tobias sat in and talk away the time.

He remembered seeing how happy his mother looked as she spoke and laughed with him. Now all of that changed. Tobias's moment of wondering off into the past was interrupted when Dolores Armando walked into the bar.

She went to the counter and placed her order to an employee. Once she got her drink she took a stool by counter being that the tables were taken up. Tobias watched her every move but tried not to make it obvious. Five minutes after she walked in, Mr. Butcher made an appearance.

He got his drink and took a stool right beside Dolores.

A minute into the awkward position, he started speaking to Dolores but Tobias could hear nothing with all the talking and laughter in the air. But he was able to study their behavior toward one another. Mr. Butcher seemed to say something that caused Dolores to giggle. They were beginning to get into a deep conversation where they laughed with one another and acted as if they were old friends.

Tobias witnessed a whole new Mr. Butcher that he had never seen before. He's only ever known the man to be aggressive and unhappy. Tobias finished his smoothie but he couldn't afford to leave. He wanted to stay as long as they stood to see the results in the end so he went to the counter to get another.

"You must be thirsty" Mr. Gibson said when Tobias asked for another mango smoothie. "It's not that. The mango smoothie is really good today. It always is."

When Mr. Gibson left to prepare another smoothie, Dolores said, "I have never seen you here before. I didn't even see you when I came in. I guess it's because you're just as ordinary as everyone else." She waved her arm which was decorated with bracelets to the people.

"It's only because of all that blue and jewels that you stand out, princesa. Otherwise you would be as ordinary as everyone else." As he spoke Mr. Butcher glared all the time at him. "I don't think so young man," Dolores said with a bit of heat. "Unlike you Americans who look the same, I'm a Spanish beauty who stands out among the crowd. Everyone whom I've met has said that I look beautiful."

"Not everyone. I haven't said that."

"Why do I need to hear it from you?" "Enough. Tobias, mind your business and scoot away from us. You disturbed a very pleasant conversation." "I don't recall you ever exchanging pleasant conversations with anyone" Tobias said. "Watch that mouth," Mr. Butcher said in a low and dangerous voice. "One day it's going to get you in serious danger and you will wish that you never opened it."

"Is that a threat?" and Tobias scooted away quickly before Mr. Butcher could say something.

Tobias ended up staying at the bar for an hour and half as Mr. Butcher and Dolores didn't seem in a hurry to depart. At one point Mr. Butcher appeared to be talking about Tobias himself for he side-eyed him along with Dolores.

At last they departed with a friendly farewell.

On their way out Mr. Butcher stopped and said something to Dolores. Dolores smiled and answered to whatever he said. Tobias was home early so he father was still at work. He gave quality time to Brutus who seemed to miss Anne for he was laying on her spot in what used to her's and Bennett's bed. To lighten his dog's mood, he took him for a short walk and then kept him occupied with a bone.

Assured that Brutus was okay, Tobias was finally able to go to his room. He added the incident at Paradise Beverage Bar to his record of the Pristine Hills Murder where he would write every development of the case.

With nothing else to do, he got in bed early without supper but with a mind full of his goal to seek vengeance.

11

CHAPTER 11

It was over breakfast the following morning that Bennett told Tobias of something that caused goosebumps to crawl all over his arms. They were having their bread and cheese while Brutus chewed down chunks of raw meat. "Toby, are you going out today?" Bennett asked.

"I haven't decided. It depends on the course of my day" Tobias replied. "Well, if you do you must be cautious. Yesterday while I was at work I noticed a man who seemed to be following me on his trap. I couldn't confirm he was following me until I stopped at Comfort Zone for lunch and he did the same.

When I finished eating, I didn't leave the diner instantly because I wanted to see what would he do. He waited for a bit and ordered a tea before finally giving in and leaving. If you go out today, be sure that no one follows you home. Whoever killed your mother seems to have something against us also. These people don't mean good to us, Toby, and we must take precautions."

"What was the man wearing? Did you see his face?" "He wore a long coat and broad-brimmed hat. He was about six feel tall. The entire time he held his face down allowing the shadow of the brim to cover his identity." "What was the color of his horse?" "Black but it's unlikely you will recognize him by the horse. Horses look the same. You should recognize him by his manner of moving about."

Tobias stood silent for a moment thinking what could Anne's killer have against her and her family.

Then it sparked in his mind like a light bulb. "The day before mom was killed she told me of her gold and property which I'll inherit when I graduate from college. She was stressing over the matter of a robbery or a scandal more than necessary.

I asked her if she feared that would happen in the future and she said she would've warned me if she knew that would happen.

She explained that she only feared something like that because it happened to her mother whom she inherited the gold from. An evil-hearted servant in the house stole her will but the police recovered it.

I think whoever is after us could be that servant or perhaps some-one else that mom feared was going to create trouble."

"She would've warned us if she knew the future held trouble."

"I know but she seemed really anxious over the subject."

"We might have to leave this house and neighborhood for good."

"What?"

"You heard me."

"I'm not leaving till the police find the killer and I meet them face to face."

"And just what are you going to do when you meet a murderer? Are you even aware that the person you will meet is a killer? Did you think that I was going to let you do something to a murderer who will just kill you right there?"

"He can't kill me with police there and plus he won't even have a weapon."

"I didn't realize just how innocent you are, Toby. You don't know that murderers have the knowledge of how to break someone's neck. That's killing without a weapon. When they find the murderer, you can say whatever you like with bars separating you guys. I'm not letting you in a room with a killer."

"Whatever you say."

Tobias rose from the breakfast table and started out of the kitchen. "What do mean by that?" Bennett turned around. "You don't control me," Tobias said. "I'm not going to remind you again. I'm twenty. One. Years. Old." "This is not controlling you, Toby—

"Stop saying my name!" "I'm doing my job as a father to keep you safe! Do you realize what just happened to your mother and that whoever killed her means no good for us? You're being stubborn!"

Tobias walked out and slammed the front door behind him. He was steaming with anger and frustration so he sucked in deep breaths as he walked to Mr. Greyson's house. When he arrived he found Natasha by the rose bushes watering them with a hose.

Her face lit up at the sight of Tobias. Tobias smiled and walked up to her. "You're always a bright sight on my dull days" he said.

Natasha looked down shyly for a brief moment. "What brings you here?" "You first and your father second. I wanted to see you and I needed to speak with your father." "I'll get him for you" Natasha said. Tobias sat in the living room and five minutes later Natasha returned with her father.

"Natasha, please make me a tea. What do you want?"

"I'll have a tea." "Two teas please, my darling." "Yes Father." "Talk to me" Mr. Greyson said sitting down in an armchair. "There's three things I need to tell you about" Tobias said. "I'm listening."

Tobias started with the incident yesterday at Paradise Beverage Bar. During his story Natasha came with the tea. He then went on to tell Mr. Greyson of the stranger who followed his father and then what his mother told him the day before her murder.

He also mentioned where Dolores acted stank with him in saying that he was just as ordinary as everyone else. She and Anne were acquaintance and never had she acted that way toward him.

Mr. Greyson took the bar incident into consideration but he didn't say anything about it. He did state his opinion on the other things Tobias told him of.

"The person or persons who killed your mother mean no good to you and your father. It's either they want the gold or it's something else. It's unlikely that the servant who attempted the robbery would show up again for the same gold for that was two decades ago and more. If your mother told you that she would've warned you of future trouble, then I don't think she was afraid of something happening. I will however report this all to the police."

"What happened with the strange men?" Tobias asked. "They were never spotted anywhere. We made inquiry at the train station and the man at the ticket booth sweared that no men matching their description had come. Mr. Dewey is starting to think that what you told was false." "I swear it wasn't false. I literally saw everything as clear as I see you."

"I believe you, Toby. It's them who don't and Jason Emery convinced them strongly that your story is false." "You believe me? Why?" "Jason Emery had a bad experience with that college student who told him a false story and now he thinks every unofficial tells lies. I believe you need to know how to differentiate between who is lying and who isn't. I can see you don't lie when you report these incidents to me."

"And how do you see that?" Tobias questioned out of curiosity. "It's easy to read when someone is lying. You must always look out for these signs: averted eye contact, blinking, stammering, pausing to think, and an unsettled posture. But some people which is rarely are experts at lying and you may not detect any of these signs."

"I'm guessing that's what detectives learn." "Indeed. There's something I want to do. I want to collect as much knowledge of your mother's past as possible and I think there's someone who might know more than you and your father." "Clara Ambrose" Tobias said.

"If you're okay with it, could I stay here? I can't have anyone knowing that I'm with you because they will tell my father and he will become angry."

"I'm okay with that. Stay away from my daughter though." "I will."

Mr. Greyson threw on his coat. "Natasha!" he called loudly. "Coming Father!" Natasha's voice said from outside. "Stay away from him" Mr. Greyson said eyeing the both of them keenly. "Okay" Natasha said.

Mr. Greyson made sure his daughter was occupied with the bushes before he left. When he disappeared from sight, Tobias stepped out of the house onto the porch and sat in a weaved chair.

"Where's your mother?" he asked. "Spending her evening with friends" Natasha replied and wiped sweat from her forehead with her arm. "You seem hot. Perhaps a ten minute break in the porch will be good."

"You're good" Natasha said. She went around to the porch. "Would you like a glass of lemonade?"

"That sounds good for a hot day." Natasha rang for the maid and told her to prepare two cold glasses of lemonade. The maid returned in twenty minutes with the lemonade. "Can I ask you a question?" Tobias asked. "Go ahead." "How did you overcome the death of your dog? The little Pomeranian from your drawing."

"When Rosy died, it was hard. It was my first time experiencing the tragedy of loss. I let myself grieve because the body and spirit needs to. Holding in grief, sadness, or pain results in a cold, hard, and inconsiderate heart. And even emotionless. But you can't spend forever grieving. It doesn't mean you forget the thing or person, it just means that you need to find that courage to keep going with the rhythm of life.

I started implying my normal and daily routine to my days slow by slow till it was fully implied. Work and studying helps distract the mind and heart from grief.

It helped but there would come times when I felt an ache or tears would sting my eyes when I looked at the drawing of my little Rosy.

I would have to remind myself that it was better for her to pass than to keep living in pain and suffering every day. I overcame my grief but I never forgot her. I miss her every day of my life." Tobias took Natasha's words into consideration and made sure to hold onto them.

Mr. Greyson returned with little to say.

Though Miss Ambrose was with Anne for many years, nothing out of the ordinary happened that would relate to her murder save the incident of the attempted robbery.

Tobias left without Mr. Greyson knowing that he and Natasha spoke. It was on his way home that he learned he was being followed.

The man was wearing a long coat and a hat just like his father described.

He kept his head low allowing the shadow of his brimmed hat to hide his face.

Tobias's heart was pumping with creeping fear. The man's six feet tall figure topped with the hat stuck out from the horde of people and it was hard to miss.

Tobias hurried on ahead until he lost the man. Before going up to the front door, he looked around to make sure the man was gone. Once assured he was nowhere in sight, he went to his house.

12

CHAPTER 12

For the next few days Tobias started trying to imply his normal routine to his life. It was harder done than said. He would get up as soon as dawn broke and have breakfast as well as feed Brutus. Brutus had his morning walks and a game a of fetch with a stick. The dog was then ready for his morning nap and this would allow Tobias to do some studying.

He begun reviewing his notes from college for when the time came to return.Afternoon was lunch time and Tobias added something extra to his and Brutus's afternoon. Aware of the impending danger that surrounded him every time he went out, he begun training Brutus to be a guard dog who reacted if someone attacked him.

Over the days Brutus's body was turning into muscle and he started losing his flabby self.Tobias was giving Brutus a rest day and so took him to the woods so he could play in the stream. It was his favorite spot since a puppy.

Tobias sat on a log and watched his dog splash around and play with a stick. "Brutus, are you having fun?" Tobias called out. Brutus turned at his name but that excited expression suddenly melted away.

A furious fire sprung in his amber eyes and gave out a ferocious bark. He sprang out of the stream and came running at Tobias. Tobias turned around only to find a man behind him. The man withdrew a silver pistol from his pocket. Tobias froze but Brutus didn't. "Brutus! Stop!"

Brutus halt in his footsteps and growled aggressively at the man. "Who are you? What do you want?" Tobias asked the man in his boldest voice.

"On your knees," the man said. "Hands up. Don't move." The man put his pistol back and withdrew a piece of rope. He grabbed Tobias's arms and pulled back.In that moment, Tobias hurled around and elbowed the man in his rib-cage. He got on his feet and threw a punch into the masked face of his opponent.

The man regained his balance and sense before seizing Tobias by the arm, yanking him forward, and kneeing him in the stomach. This maneuver snatched the breath from Tobias's lungs.

Brutus barked nonstop with great aggression and ferociousness. He attempted to come forward but Tobias raised his hand quickly which told the dog to stay back. He was afraid that Brutus might get hurt. The man kept kneeing Tobias in the stomach. He then threw him to the forest floor. Tobias stood laying there breathless and beat. The man whose figure was like six feet tall walked up to Tobias and placed his boot on his chest.

"Who are you?" Tobias asked between rapid breaths. "What do you want from me?" "You have seen things, young man, that you weren't supposed to see."

"You mean the men in the woods?"

Tobias seized the man's leg, wrapped his around it, and twisted it until a sickening crack was heard. The man screamed in agony and fell over. Tobias nearly got up but his determined opponent grasped the collar of his coat and pulled him down. Tobias slid out of the coat and jumped to his feet.

The man stood up in an unbalanced manner for his leg was injured and pulled his gun out from his pocket.

Tobias placed his fingers between his teeth and gave out a whistle. "Shoot me" he said.

The man was about to bring his pistol up when Brutus leaped onto his back and knocked him over. The pistol flew out of the man's hand and Tobias caught it.

Tobias raised his hand and Brutus backed off. The man groaned and attempted to rise but he was weak, injured, and beaten.

"Over on your back," Tobias said while aiming the pistol at him. He then kneeled down and put the pistol to the man's forehead before ripping the mask off.

The man looked to be somewhere in his late thirties. His white face and icy blue eyes had an aggressive look that made him look like a someone people would avoid. Tobias took his hat off which revealed the man's hair color to be blond. "Who are you? Who sent you?"

"I'd rather die than tell you anything."

"You must be a loyal dog to your master." Tobias didn't know what hit him, but a sudden sharp pain pierced through his side.He cried out in agony and got off the man. When he brought his hand to his side he found a knife stuck in his flesh. Tobias sucked in a deep breath before pulling it out. The man gave a wicked laugh before attacking Tobias again.

They rolled over like a barrel bringing the man over Tobias. Tobias used the knife to stab the man in the heart. It was a bloody scene. Crimson liquid squirted everywhere and all over Tobias's clothes.

The man gasped and dropped to the ground. Tobias lie beside the dying man while sucking in deep and rapid breaths. When he turned his head the man was dead.

Tobias got up rapidly when he realized that he just took a life. Brutus walked up to the dead body and gave it a sniff. Tobias stared with an utterly shocked and blank mind. "I just killed someone" he whispered. A moment later he was panickily washing splattered blood off his face in the stream.

He then took Brutus and started running from the woods, but he was kind of limp on his left side due to the wound. Tobias took off in a run to home. Brutus barked at the crowds of people making way for Tobias. Everyone shot him confused and strange expressions, but Tobias could care less at the moment about what people thought of him. He just killed a man and the stab on his side was staining his shirt in blood.

Tobias knocked rapidly at the door and his father who was having a day off from work opened it. "Tobias?" Bennett said.

Tobias brushed past his father and hurried to the living room. "Tobias, what happened?" Bennett went after his son.

Tobias took off his jacket revealing a blood-soaked button-up shirt. "Oh my goodness," Bennett said staring with a pair of horrified eyes. "Clara! Get the doctor!" In just a few seconds Clara the maid, Julia the cook, and Stella the housekeeper were in the living room. Clara rushed out to fetch the local doctor.

Julia went to the kitchen to bring a glass of water for Tobias. Stella aided Bennett in helping Tobias take off his shirt so they could clean up the blood. Tobias was sweating and shaking all over. He couldn't seem to concentrate on his surroundings or what was going on. When Julia brought the water, he gulped it down like he had never drank before. The rest he suddenly threw on his face.

"Tobias, you need to sit on the sofa so we can clean- "I'm hot" Tobias cut him off. He pushed past him and went to the kitchen when he turned on the faucet and begun throwing water on his face. Brutus was in the background barking stressfully and following Tobias. "Toby, are you okay? You need to speak to me" Bennett said. "Do I look okay?" Tobias turned around to yell. "Why would you ask if I'm okay? Does this look okay? I'm having a panic attack! I'm hot, I'm sweating, I'm shaking, and my senses are unclear!"

"The doctor is here" Julia came in the kitchen to say. Clara entered the house with the doctor following. Eric Shawn was the family doctor who they called every time they needed medical aid, so he was familiar with the family and the house.

"Oh my, what is happening in here?" Mr. Shawn asked. Bloody clothes were laying on the living room floor, the women appeared nervous, Brutus was barking, and Tobias was acting mad. In a minute Mr. Shawn had the situation under control. Tobias calmed down and was laying on the sofa while the doctor cleaned and stitched his wound together.

When Mr. Shawn finished the job, he was dismissed. Bennett ordered the women to give him and Tobias a private moment in the living room. "Tell me what happened" he said. Tobias remained silent with Brutus beside him next to the sofa. He stared at the ceiling in complete silence.

"Let me guess. You got into a fight?" Bennett said. When Tobias said nothing, Bennett thought for a moment before it came to his mind. "Was he following you? Did you go up to him to ask him why and then you guys fought?"

Tobias didn't answer but a knock came to the door. Bennett rose to open it. "Mr. Emery? Mr. Greyson? Police? What's going on?" he asked. "We believe your son is responsible for the murder of Jack Oberon" Jason Emery said.

"Wait, wait. What in the universe is going on? Who is Jack Oberon? And Toby, why is the police at my door saying you committed murder?" Bennett was confused, lost, and nervous. He moved aside from the front door letting Jason Emery, Dwight Greyson, and the police inside. The women were peeking at the scene from the hallway. "Tobias, tell us what happened" Mr. Greyson said. "Can I know who informed the police?" Tobias asked.

"Some random woman. She reported that she saw you running from the woods with great fear and panic on your face and your dog was acting aggressive toward people. She said she thought something wasn't right about the scene and assumed that something happened in those secluded woods."

Mr. Greyson took a chair beside the sofa. "Tell me what happened. You come clean now and you will be clear in the end. You come with lies and you will be in trouble in the end."

Tobias sucked in a deep breath. "Ever since my father told me of the man who followed him, I didn't feel safe so I started a training program with Brutus so he would play the role of a guard dog. I decided that today I would give him rest for he was training hard. He loves the stream in the woods, so I took him there.

He was playing and I was watching him from a log. At point I called his name and asked him if he was having fun. When he looked at me, his expression changed suddenly. He began growling and then launched out of the stream. I turned around and there was a tall man standing behind me. He pulled a pistol from his coat and at the sight of it I commanded Brutus to stop. The man told me to get on my knees and raise my hands.

When he started tying my hands with a rope, I hurled around and elbowed him in the ribcage. One thing led to another and before I knew it, I was engaged in my first fight.

At one point I asked the man who was he and what did he want from me. He said that I had seen things I wasn't supposed to and then I mentioned the men in the woods. He didn't say anything which told me that was it. We fought violently and he stabbed me here. I pulled the knife out and kept it in my possession.

When he was over me, I stabbed it in his heart. Mr. Greyson, I would never kill anyone. I swear. But I didn't know what to do at that point. I was fighting for my life. The man had a gun and knife in possession. He was probably going to kill me."

"I believe you, Tobias," Mr. Greyson said. "You will not be charged with the murder because it was a life and death situation." Tobias was able to breath again hearing those words. "Who is that man?" he asked.

"We don't know much about him except what we learned. His name is Jack Oberon, and he works for the construction industry in Pristine Hills." "That doesn't even make sense. What does a construction man have against me?"

"I don't know," Mr. Greyson said and looked to Bennett. "Mr. James, you worked in the construction industry in the past. Did know of a Jack Oberon?" "No, I didn't. I had friends but none of them from what I remember was named Jack Oberon."

"Alright, we'll let you know of further developments." Mr. Greyson said and gave Tobias a sneaky wink. Tobias knew what he meant. 'We'll talk when you come.'

When the detectives and police left the house, there was a silence between Bennett and Tobias. Bennett broke the silence by saying, "What did I tell you about the woods? That man could've killed you instead of you killing him. I wish I could send you back to college because you seriously need your days filled with occupations."

"Why do you wish?" Tobias asked. "I didn't want to tell you because I didn't want you stressing, but money is low and I can't afford to send you back for a while. When your poor mother was alive, we worked together. But now I'm working alone."

13

CHAPTER 13

Tobias found sleep was a long distance away when he got in bed that night. His mind and spirit were affected by the traumatizing events that occurred in his day. He couldn't believe that he killed someone, but he had to keep telling himself that it was a matter of life and death. If he didn't act, the man would've killed him.

Brutus seemed a bit disturbed also, so he slept on the rug beside Tobias's bed. Since finding sleep was impossible, Tobias occupied his mind with gathering every fact and development of the case and spinning them into a theories, but none of them made sense. He eventually fell asleep and awoke the following morning with the intention of going to Detective Greyson's house.

Arriving at Mr. Greyson's house he found Natasha riding one of their two horses around the estate. At the sight of Tobias, she ordered the horse to stop, and she jumped off. "I've never seen him before" Natasha said. Her speech was directed at Brutus who stood beside Tobias on a leash. "His name is Brutus."

"He's so cute" Natasha squealed and ruffled up the big dog's fur and ears. Brutus wagged his tail and tried to lick her face. "How are you?" she asked rising to face Tobias. "I'm doing great" Tobias replied. "Tobias, be truthful with me. My father told me what happened yesterday. How are you doing great after that?"

"Natasha!" a voice screamed from somewhere high. Natasha and Tobias saw Dona Greyson by the window on the second floor of their house. "Get away from him! He didn't come to see you! He came for your father!"

"What's the problem with me saying hi to her?" Tobias asked, walking forward. "Do you not allow her to say hi to anyone?"

"Don't be a sassy pants with me," Mrs. Greyson said with some heat. "When I say to stay away from my daughter, you respect it and keep your behind away. Do you understand?"

"Yes ma'am."

Tobias tied Brutus's leash to the fencing that surrounded the porch and Natasha let him in the house.

"I will get my father" she said. A minute later she returned with her father, and he dismissed her to speak with Tobias privately. "I'm glad you got the meaning of my wink yesterday," Mr. Greyson said. "I wanted to speak with you about the case as well as the police's theoretical story. And you can share your theories if you have any."

"I don't have one," Tobias said. "But what did the police say about what I did?" "Mr. Dewey let it go being that you killed the man in life defense. That has been pushed aside so you have no reason to worry about future charges. After that happened however, Mr. Dewey did hold a long meeting in the conference room where the detectives and police who are engaged with the case attended. We were there for hours putting together the facts and events and spinning them into theories.

The theory I suggested goes something like this. The people involved with the murder include Wendy, Dolores, Mr. Wilson, Jack

Oberon, and those men from the woods. I believe Jack Oberon is the man with the beard who was going to be paid to do the last task and perhaps what he did yesterday was the last task. Before I lay the theory out, you should know why we suspect Mr. Wilson to be involved with the murder. Mr. Wilson is a former criminal."

"Are you serious?" Tobias started.

"His original name is Fletcher Damon. His crime record states that he killed thirty-seven people, robbed forty-two houses and shops in total, and kidnapped thirty-eight young girls and children in total. He was arrested by the police five years ago and had his sentence of jail. Ever since he kept his promise to never commit crime again and he hasn't. The reason for his attitude has to do with the effect of murdering and kidnapping. Those things traumatize the mind and spirit, and you experienced it yesterday. I don't think the poor fellow healed from his past and the sad part is that he has no one to help him.

What makes it hard for the police to see what he has been recently doing is the fact that he has no maids or housekeepers for us to interrogate.

This is what we think happened, but the future will reveal the truth. Wendy started planning the murder five years ago. She started by announcing that she no longer cared for your father and that her grudge on your mother faded. She apologized to her husband and told him that she loved him. She had her family as witnesses to prove this. She waited for five years to make it look real. When five years went by, she resumed her scheme.

Her best friend is Dolores, so she felt safe in telling her what she was planning.

I'm starting to think there might be a connection between Dolores and Mr. Wilson after what you witnessed at the bar. Wendy informed Dolores of her plan and paid her to play her role by the window hanging laundry.

When your mother arrived in Pristine Hills and stole your father's heart from Wendy, Wendy started plotting against her from then. She informed Dolores of her plot. It was Dolores's job to make acquaintance of your mother's so that when the time comes, it wouldn't look suspicious for her to call her name and exchange friendly conversation-

"That sounds reasonable, but the question arises: why did Wendy wait until now to put her plot into action? Why did she wait twenty-one years?" Tobias said.

"Okay, then that doesn't fit in. Let's go back to the original idea. She started plotting five years ago and the acquaintanceship between Dolores and your mother wasn't part of the plan but became an advantage for Wendy and even Dolores.

Wendy and Dolores were trying to look for a suitable shooter and Dolores suggested Mr. Wilson. Because of their close relationship he told her of his past and that's why she felt he would be good for the shooting job. On the day of the killing, Wendy went out to meet Dolores and Mr. Wilson and tell them that it was time. She then left to buy a few vegetables to make it appear that she was doing grocery shopping. Dolores was ready with a basket of wet laundry and Mr. Wilson positioned himself on the third floor of the abandoned buildings.

When Anne walked out of the building, Dolores was already hanging her laundry by the window. She called her out, exchanged friendly words, bought Mr. Wilson time, and he shot her. This theory links together well but when it comes to the men in the woods and Jack Oberon, they are another story. I feel strongly these men are enemies from Anne's past and that she never told you or your father."

"But my mom clearly said that she would have warned me of future danger." "People say things, Tobias. Perhaps she didn't think these enemies if they are, would rise from the shadows again." "So, what do these men want? And why was a construction man trying to kidnap me or kill me? Whatever he wanted to do to me."

"What I believe is that Jack Oberon is part of Anne's enemies. He followed her to Pristine Hills and went under the disguise of a construction man. Who knows? He could've been working on Anne's house when she hired men from the construction industry. The men in the woods are under a disguise just as he was. I don't know what they want but I'm about to do some research. Do you know where your mother's family resides?"

"Pennsylvania in a town called Woodland Square. The neighborhood is Redwood. She told me this a while back and said that if anything happened, I had a place to flee to."

"It's guaranteed. She feared something. There's no doubting it. Tomorrow I'm leaving to do some investigation over there. I won't be back for at least two weeks so if anything occurs, you are welcome to my house or if you feel safer going to your mother's family."

"Will there be a way for me to communicate with you? What if something out of the ordinary happens and I need to tell you as I usually do?" "I will be busy, Tobias. I don't want our letters to be discovered by the police and they find out that I have been sharing details of the case with an unofficial. If anything out of the ordinary occurs just go to Mr. Dewey."

"Okay," Tobias said looking down at his shoes. "What's wrong?" Mr. Greyson asked. "I just... Nothing."

"I won't take that as an answer." "After you told me to stay away from the case because it could get me in trouble with the police, I had it set in my mind that I wouldn't back down. I made a promise that I would avenge my mother. It has been my only priority. But I feel like I haven't done anything, and the things just come to me."

"I can imagine the anger boiling in you to avenge her, Tobias," Mr. Greyson said. "But I will give you one piece of advice that is logical and will save you trouble in the future with the police. Leave the case in the hands of the police."

"How can I do that when you guys have done nothing since the day my mother was murdered save those little interrogations?" Tobias asked. Anger was beginning to boil like a pot of water on the fire. "Every development of the case I have reported back to you occurred infront of me. The police haven't done anything. They used my evidence to form theories. What are they doing with the case? Did they just give up and haven't said anything?"

"Calm down, Tobias," said Mr. Greyson. "Stop saying my name." "The police did what they could. What else was there for them to do after the interrogations?"

"I don't want to hear it. Mr. Dewey needs to step down and someone sharper needs to step up."

"I will stop discussing the case with you if you continue speaking like this. You are clearly unaware of the trouble and even dangers you will find yourself in if the police discover what you think and say of them. It's not just prison. People like you are considered harmful to the police and their reputation. They kill people like you. They have done it in the past and I was there to witness it."

Tobias calmed down and stood quiet. When he spoke again, he said, "I'm sorry. Are you going to inform them?"

"No I won't. But it can't happen again. I won't be able to cover you next time."

14

CHAPTER 14

Tobias got in bed that night with a hundred thoughts regarding his conversation earlier but one goal set: avenge his mother. That's all he wanted, and he wasn't going to let any obstacles get in his way. Bennett stopped by his bedroom as was his usual. "How's your wound healing?" he asked.

"It's healing fine."

"I'm glad to hear. I just wanted to tell you that I'm sorry if I haven't been there for you as much I should. I'm going through it just like you, but I put on a strong mask. I wonder what my purpose in life will be after you graduate college and start your own life."

"Life will be different by then. It will bring you and me opportunities and changes."

"You're right. Goodnight, Toby."

"Night, dad."

When night was it's darkest and deadest was when the predators decided to target their heedless prey. Brutus awoke in the middle of the night to the smell of smoke. His keen sense of hearing picked up the sound of cackling fire. And so he set off the alarm with loud barks that rang throughout the house.

Tobias jumped from his sleep. "Brutus, what ha- where's that smoke coming from?" When he looked at his window, fiery orange flames were blocking the view.

"Toby!" came the panicked voice of Bennett. "We must leave now! The house is surrounded in fire!"

"I can't leave like this. There's my gold. I need to get it." "Come on. Hurry."

Bennett and Tobias started for the bedroom. "Clara, take Brutus and the others and leave. We will be with you guys in a moment." Clara nodded nervously and started off with Julia, Stella, and the dog. Bennett and Tobias went the bedroom.

"The safe is behind the closet" Tobias said. With the help of his father, they pushed against the closet to expose the safe. Bennett stopped to cough and catch his breath. The smoke and ashes were getting to his lungs. "We need wet cloths" Tobias said.

From Natasha's bedroom window on the second floor of her family's house, she spotted the flames and smoke burning bright against the night sky. "Mother, there's a fire!" she cried running to her parents' room.

Tobias and his father were able to continue pushing the closet with wet cloths tied around their mouth and nose like a mask.

When the metal safe was exposed, Tobias rushed over to the vase of flowers on his mother's table. He dumped the dirt out onto the floor and scattered it carelessly in search for the key. It wasn't long before his eye caught a silver shine among the soil.

He opened the safe and for the first time set his eyes on what was to be his property soon. But something wasn't right. Atop the pile of gold was a black, oval-shaped, gemstone. Tobias didn't recall his mother saying that an Opal gemstone was part of his inheritance.

But he didn't have time for questions. He and his father shoved the gold as well as the opal into a leather bag.

"We have to leave now" Bennett said, his voice muffled due to the cloth. They started out of the bedroom. Tobias snatched up his mother's wedding ring box and shoved it into the bag. The fire was fast and furious eating up a large of portion of the house's woodwork. Planks were falling from the ceiling and the flames were making their way into the rooms.

As they ran down the hallway trying to avoid planks that would fall out of nowhere, Tobias went into his bedroom to retrieve the will. "Tobias! What are you doing?"

"The will! I can't leave it!" Tobias said.

He found the will in his closet among his clothes and added it to the bag. "My record" he whispered, going over to his drawer, and pulling out a slot. He rummaged through the papers and withdrew his record of the case.

"Hurry up!" Bennett raised his voice. Bennett felt like they were in the burning house for ages because Tobias kept coming up with something important he needed to get before leaving. But at last they evacuated the house and burst through the front door. They ripped the cloths off their faces and gasped for air as if they hadn't breathed in ages. "Are you guys okay?" Clara asked rushing over to them.

"My lungs" Bennett said a series of heavy coughs following. Everyone's attention including the spectators who emerged from their homes was snatched by the clapping of many horse hooves.

Policemen in their hansoms were riding at full speed before whipping their horses to stop. Tobias recognized Dwight Greyson, Jason Emery, and Frank Dewey. "Get away from the fire!" Jason Emery raised his voice loudly for everyone to hear. "Connect the hose! Get buckets of water!"

By now half of the house fell in destruction due to the raging fire. The policemen were at work putting out the fire with a nearby hose and pales of water that the people were bringing them. The battle between man and an element of nature was no easy one.

The water seemed to be fueling the flames or perhaps a better way to put it is making them angry, for when the water touched them they rose and burned brighter. Tobias stared in despair all the time unaware of what was going on around him.

He had not even a hint that Natasha was there with her mother. He found himself focused on his future property that was being eaten by the fire. "Tobias, Tobias," a distant voice called. "Are you okay?" He jumped from space-out when someone shook him by the shoulder. It was Natasha who appeared very concern.

He stared at her blankly. "Tobias, speak to me" she said. "I don't have anything to say," he said. "I just lost everything."

"I'm sorry" Natasha said and embraced him in a hug. Tobias returned it. When dawn broke, the fire was put out. Natasha stood with Tobias the whole time, speaking encouraging words to him. The damage of the house was revealed when the fire was out. The white and grey house was now black as coal and the whole second floor was ashes.

"The fire is out," Mr. Greyson said. He and the policemen were wet, tired, and dirty due to the flying ashes. Pristine Hills was cloaked in a cloud of smoke giving the neighborhood a hazy and mysterious vibe. "It's a blessing no one got injured or died."

"That's a blessing?" Tobias stood up. "What about my house?"

His voice grabbed the attention of the police and the people. "This was my house left to me by my mother! This was to be mines and now it's destroyed and unrepairable! I can't even sell or repair it! I swear infront of you all by my flesh and bones that I will find whoever killed my mother and whoever has ill-wishes against me and give them something greater than what they did to me! I don't want to hear anybody's sympathies and sorry for what happened! Not even from you, Natasha! I don't regret a single-

"Tobias, cut it out!" Bennett stepped forward when he saw his son getting out of hand. But he wasn't expecting what he got when he approached his son. Tobias pushed his father infront of the crowd. The crowd gasped in shock and Natasha stared in disbelief. "Now you know why I tell you stay away from him" her mother said. Detective Greyson and Emery rushed forward to put Tobias under control. Clara got Bennett's back as he nearly fell.

"Get off me!" Tobias yelled at the detectives. Frank Dewey walked forward with a grave look on his old face. "Mr. James, I hope you don't mind us taking your son to the station for a bit" he said. "Take him" Bennett said.

It wasn't long before the police hansoms pulled up at the DPA department. Tobias was led to a room on the second floor and placed in a chair.

Detective Dwight and Jason took positions by the front door and one officer was ordered to stand outside. Mr. Dewey's face appeared grave and serious which meant no good. "You plan on finding the killer yourself. What a brave act on your side" he said. "I will find the killer" Tobias said.

"Are you aware of what you are doing? What are you getting yourself into?" "I'm aware of it all and I don't give a dog's vomit about it."

Mr. Dewey violently grabbed Tobias by the collar of his jacket and shook him. "You don't know what you are doing and what are you getting yourself into. People like you think they are some sort of hero, but the result of their little missions is death by the hands of the police. The government nor the police will tolerate your behavior and they will not have patience with it either. You either get your emotions together or die with the blame on them."

When Tobias was released, he ran for the woods. He ran through the trees until arriving at the stream and dropping to the ground. He was shaken from fear and shock. He stopped for a moment to breath and calm down emotionally. His eyes landed on the watch on his wrist, and he took it off to read the message in the back. I love you to the moon and back ~ Mom.

Tobias broke into a sob. Tears streamed from his eyes and dropped to the soil. His head rose to look up at the hazy sky that clouded with smoke. "I need you, mom," he said. "I can't do this anymore. I lost you, I killed a man, and the house is destroyed. Who is after me and dad? Why didn't you ever tell us if you knew?"

"Tobias are you here?" called the voice of Bennett. Tobias said nothing but allowed his father to find him. When Bennett spotted him, he rushed to his son in concern and worry. He kneeled beside him and put his arm on him. Tobias fell into his father's chest and cried freely.

A meeting was held in Dwight's house which included his wife and daughter with their maids and housekeepers, Bennett and Tobias with their maid, housekeeper, and cook. "Tobias, will you not go to your mother's family's house?" Dwight asked.

"I will not go until the police recover the schemers behind the killing of my mother and everything else that has occurred afterwards," Tobias replied calm but sternly. "No one, not even the police or my father, will force to me to leave Pristine Hills. I am my own man and I make my own decisions."

"My only priority though is to be certain that you are in a safe place away from these people who have ill-wishes against us" Bennett told Tobias.

"But I will not leave the neighborhood." "You made it clear, Toby." "Alright then, it's clear Tobias will not leave the neighborhood," Dwight said. "Do you have any ideas, Mr. James?"

"I don't know where else to put him because he wants to be so stubborn. Anne's family's house is the best option because in the meantime I don't have enough to pay rent for an apartment. I don't even have money to continue paying for his college."

"Tobias, are you really going to make it hard for your father? Where do you want to go? Would you like to sleep on the street?" "I will if I have to."

Tobias's manner was stern, cold, and dead serious. He kept his arms folded on his chest and his hard eyes glaring at everyone. "I have an idea," Dwight said. "Before I lay it out however, I would like to say something for everyone to hear. Tobias and I have met several times so far to discuss the case and he has reported every single unordinary incident that he witnessed.

I have seen the kind of man he is, strong witted, courageous, no-quitter, and good hearted. I would say that he and I have gotten close enough to be friends. He is a good young man and therefore he will stay in my house under my protection till this case is closed. Of course, you as well as Mr. James."

"I appreciate your kindness, Mr. Greyson," Bennett said. "But I can't do this. I will not put a burden by staying in another man's house when we have a free place to go to. That's shameful for me and I'm sure you can understand."

Tobias stood up from the armchair in which he had been seated. "You can go, and I will come to you when the case is closed" Tobias said, facing his father sternly. "I will not leave you in this neighborhood" Bennett said. "Fine, then stay." When Bennett said nothing, Dwight spoke. "I happen to have an extra bedroom upstairs which wasn't needed and so it remains unused. You two can have it and stay there still the case is closed."

"As to you women," Bennett said to Clara, Julia, and Stella. "You guys are no longer in my hire and are free to return to your families."

The evening found Tobias sitting on the step of the porch after helping with furnishing the room lightly. He watched Brutus play in the grass and chew on a stick. So drowned in his thoughts was he that when a hand touched his shoulder he jumped in a startled manner. "I'm sorry," Dwight said. "I didn't mean to scare you." "It's okay" Tobias said as Dwight sat next to him.

"I'm sorry about everything." "About what? You did nothing, Tobias."

"I'm sorry about not listening to your warning regarding the police. Mr. Dewey threatened me just as you said they would. I'm sorry about my stubbornness in not wanting to leave because now I'm just an extra burden on you and your family. I want to know why you are taking all this for me?"

"When I was your age, my mother passed away from cancer. She and my father were divorced. My father didn't care when she died because he was a bad man who thought of himself only and associated himself with bad people. He didn't care to send me a letter when she died. I had no one to be by my side. I had friends but friends are not going to give you that kind of support. It's family. I didn't have that. I had no choice but to move on with my life and make it through alone."

"I'm sorry" Tobias said.

"Don't be. As the old saying goes, life is unfair. But it is what it is. What can we do about it."

"What do you think of the fire?"

"Someone made it without a doubt. They poured gasoline around the house and strangely left the front door clear as if they wanted you all to escape. They then threw a match or something like that on the gasoline. There's no other way that the fire could've started. One it encircled the house save the front door. Two it was burning from outside not inside. Three it's impossible for a fire to spread around an entire in just a matter of seconds. Only gasoline can trigger that kind of effect."

"It confuses me that whoever made it intended for us to escape. What was the point of that fire then?"

"I'm just as confused as you are. You know that you can't hold that gold around with you though. Whoever is after you and your father might set eyes on it. I suggest putting it in a safe in the bank."

"Speaking of the gold, when I opened the safe, there was an Opal gemstone sitting at the top of the pile. My mother never told me that Opal would be in my inheritance as well. It's big and worth hundreds of dollars."

"She never told you about it?"

"No, never. I was confused when I saw it."

"The plot thickens" Dwight said, staring ahead.

15

✦

CHAPTER 15

Dinner with Dwight's family was silent and quick. Tobias washed up for bed right after while his father stood downstairs speaking with Dwight. Brutus got comfortable beside the carpet. An hour after he was in bed, his father joined him in the room. Bennett hung his dressing gown on the door and sat in his mattress which was what they had.

He looked at his son who lay in his mattress staring thoughtfully at the ceiling. He cleared his throat to grab his attention. "What are you thinking about?" Bennett asked.

"Nothing" Tobias said, looking at his father. "You're thinking about something. I can see it in your eyes."

"I regret earlier, how I reacted and what I said especially what I said to Natasha. That's not the first time I've had a raging outburst infront of people and the police."

"I'm glad you regret it, because I wanted to tell you that you need to stop those outbursts. They embarrass me greatly. I don't want people knowing I'm the father of this crazy son."

"I'm sorry. I will stop that, but it will be difficult."

"I'm surprised by you today. I didn't know you were visiting a detective's house behind my back. Why did you lie about hanging out with Ben? You could've just told me the truth."

"It's not like you would agree with me visiting a detective. You didn't even agree with my secret investigation of the case."

"That's illegal. Did you expect me to support you and then get in trouble with you in the end?"

"You have a point there. What do you want me to say about visiting Mr. Greyson?"

"I'm not happy with it. I don't want you getting involved with official matters and associating yourself with detectives. Everything you say is reported back to the police and if they find something they don't like, you will be in major trouble. Not only will you be in trouble, but they will look at me being that I'm the father."

"Mr. Greyson doesn't tell anyone what we say among each other. As a matter of a fact, our conversations are to be kept a secret. He doesn't even allow his family in the living room when we speak. I'm not associating myself with official matters. All I do is report unordinary occurrences that I witnessed, and he reports them back to the police. We discuss the case when new developments rise and then spin our personal theories."

"If it's only that, then that's fine. Now what is it between you and Natasha?"

"We're friends. What happens between us is none of your business."

"Well, it will be my business if you decide on marriage."

"It's too early for that."

"How old is she?"

"Nineteen."

"What is she like?"

"She's sharp, brilliant, and amazing. Now enough with this subject."

"Alright, I won't ask anything else. Mr. Greyson suggested earlier after dinner when we were speaking that I give the gold to the bank for safe keeping."

"He told me the same thing."

"I think it's our only option. Carrying this precious bundle around isn't a good idea when hounds are on our track. I'll take care of that tomorrow. You and I need to sleep. We've been up since yesterday midnight due to that catastrophe. Night, Toby."

"Night."

The rising sun signaled the break of dawn. Its golden rays penetrated hazily through the cloud of smoke that hung over Pristine Hills due to the recent fire at Tobias's house.

Tobias blinked the sleep from his eyes and looked across at Bennett's bed. The bed was empty, and the leather bag of gold was gone, which told him that his father rose early.

Brutus noticed his beloved human awake, so he walked over to him. He whimpered happily as if saying good morning and tried to lick Tobias's face. "Let's go get breakfast" Tobias said.

Before washing himself up or having breakfast, Tobias served Brutus first. He chopped the piece of red meat into bite size chunks and put them in the bowl. He then refilled Brutus's water bowl and placed the bowls in the corner of the kitchen. Brutus ran over to his breakfast hungrily and started gobbling up the meat. "Slowly. You don't want to choke or vomit," Tobias said. "Well, it's not like you understand me."

Tobias returned upstairs to get in bathroom before someone else did because the household was beginning to awake. When he exited the bathroom, Mr. Greyson appeared carrying two bags toward the staircase. "What are you doing?" Tobias asked.

"I packed my bags for my trip to Pennsylvania. My train will be here in an hour."

"You'll be gone for two weeks then."

"Correct. Remember to report any unordinary occurrences to Mr. Dewey but do not make it appear that you did some sort of secret investigation. And don't do that. You've already seen what happens."

"I won't. I learnt my lesson."

"I'm glad. Go have breakfast. It should be ready."

Dwight predicted correctly for when Tobias walked in the kitchen, the cook laid out two boiled eggs, toast, and a coffee. He consumed his breakfast hungrily and afterwards washed the plate and mug. He also cleaned up after Brutus.

"You wanna go out, Brutus" Tobias said. Brutus licked his lips from breakfast and wagged his tail. He exited the kitchen with Brutus following and found Dwight saying goodbye to his wife and daughter. He kept his distance out of respect.

"How long will you be away?" Natasha asked. "Two weeks, darling. No longer than that." Natasha hugged her father and then he turned to his wife. They embraced one another and he kissed her on the cheek. When they disengaged the hug, Dwight saw Tobias. "Don't do something crazy" he said, smiling amusingly. Tobias smiled. "I won't. You can trust me."

Dwight departed from his family to get in the trap which waited outside.

"Come now," Dona told her daughter. "You need to get ready for another day at Blue Lake University." Natasha gloomily followed her mother. Tobias looked at her in sympathy as he regretted what he told her yesterday after the fire was put out. She hadn't approached him since he said that. Tobias let Brutus out onto the estate to do his business. He then went upstairs to fetch his coat and hat before leaving the house. "Stay there," Tobias said when Brutus tried to follow him. "I'm just going to get something. I'll be back."

Brutus watched Tobias walk away while whimpering with pinned ears. Tobias kept his face down as he walked in a hurry to his destination. He didn't want to bring attention to him as he knew people wouldn't fail to recognize that crazy man who had the outrageous burst from the fire. But not looking ahead costed him the price of crashing into someone.

Tobias looked up to learn that the person whom he crashed into was his friend Ben Hudson. It was an awkward moment as both friends stared at each other blankly.

"Ben," Tobias said. Ben shifted nervously. Tobias sensed the strange nervousness in Ben's manner, but he said nothing. "What happened to you? You disappeared since the day we were at the bar and the police came."

"Can we talk about this somewhere other than the middle of the sidewalk?" Ben asked.

Tobias and Ben went to a nearby café where they ordered tea and took a table by the glass window. "Tell me where you have been" Tobias said seriously. Ben inhaled deeply before saying, "My mother said I'm not allowed to associate myself with you anymore." "Why is that?"

"The police suspect her highly of your mother's murder because she was a former rival. She's trying to avoid any interaction with your family because she doesn't want to police thinking something or taking something in the wrong way."

"Do you agree with her?"

Ben stood silent and lowered his head. He then lifted it and looked Tobias in the eyes. "I do agree with her, and I am willing to let you go. We are no longer friends."

Tobias sucked in a deep breath. He could feel his heart burning up in anger and he knew that if he didn't suck it in, he was going to have another outburst infront of everyone in the café.

It took everything he had even hard breaths and looking away from Ben's face to control the building anger. "I should've known we weren't friends," Tobias said. "You never gave a word of sympathy when my mother was killed. You didn't show up when my house went down in flames. It's true. The times of hardship are the times that reveal who is your friend and who isn't."

Tobias rose from the chair and shoved it against the wall. He took the cup of tea and dropped it on the floor. The shatter grabbed the attention of the people in the café. Tobias walked out like nothing happened. Ben looked at the people who were staring at him. "What are you looking at?" he asked.

The people shot him strange looks before returning to their business.

Tobias was steaming up in anger as he recontinued his steps to his destination. At last he arrived at a shop that sold wigs, fake beards, fake mustaches, and all sorts of fake facial parts for disguise. He went over to the beard section and scanned over them. He spotted a short brown beard and took it to the counter.

"Is that all?" the man asked. "Yes" Tobias replied. He paid for the beard and put it in the pocket of his jacket as he exited the store. When Tobias arrived home, he exchanged his clothes for a professional looking attire. This attire included a suit, a tie, a long jacket, and a hat. As he headed for the front door again, Dona happened to be walking by.

"Where are you going out to again? And what's with the professional attire?" she asked. "I have to take care of some business" Tobias said before heading out.

He put on his fake beard and flagged down a hansom from the road. He told the driver to take him to the Pristine Hills Hospital.

The driver whipped his white mare which caused her to neigh and then take off. The hansom went flying down the street. It was a fifteen-minute ride before it pulled at the hospital. Tobias leaped out and paid the driver his fee. When the hansom rode away, he walked across the street from the hospital and started down toward the DPA department.

He pushed the wooden door open ignoring the stares of the security men. In entering the department, Tobias began having seconds thoughts of what he was doing. He had no idea what to do or where to go. Officers and policemen were everywhere. Some took the staircase to the upper floors. Others walked by with documents and folders. And a few were speaking in proximity. Tobias wasn't sure where to start but he knew he couldn't stand there because he would eventually bring attention.

To his fortune, policemen suddenly walked in with a man who wasn't a policeman. Officers on the left and right held him by the arms as they walked him in. Tobias recognized the man to be Samuel Armando. Samuel was a large and primitive man who was said to have little hygiene. He wore his black hair in a little ponytail and had a small beard. He didn't dress like a gentleman. Tobias slipped in with the other officers and followed them to wherever they were taking Samuel.

Detective Emery stopped the small group. "What's going on here?" he asked. "Mr. Armando here returned. Mr. Dewey ordered that we bring him in for questioning" said the policeman at the head of the group.

"Take him to the room," Detective Emery said. "I'll report to the chief." Tobias followed the policemen down a long hallway that was lined on either side with brown doors. The head policeman pushed open one of the doors. "Sit down" he told Samuel, pointing to the chair by the silver desk.

Five minutes found Mr. Dewey along with Detective Emery in the room. Tobias stood by the front door with another officer. Detective Emery took the opposite seat by the desk. "Have you heard of the murder of Anne James?" he asked. "Yes, my wife told me all about it" Samuel replied. "Good. I heard that you visit your sickly mother and other relatives every six months for three weeks. Your wife told me that when she asked you which state do you travel to, you refused to answer that question. Why is that?"

Samuel seemed stuck at words. He threw nervous darting glancing around the room. Tobias paid close attention to the way he carried himself and the tone of his voice when he did speak. "I don't have to tell her or you where my family lives," Samuel finally said. "It's my right."

Detective Emery stared at the large figure. "There's only one reason someone wouldn't give away a simple thing. They are lying."

"I'm not lying!" Samuel kicked his chair and slapped his large brown hand on the desk. Detective Emery didn't give a reaction. He sat calmly in his chair and looked at Samuel with relaxed eyes. "Then why don't you tell us where your family lives? That'll prove it."

"Listen here. If you believe that I'm guilty of the murder of this woman, then that is your problem. If I know I'm not guilty, I'm not afraid of the police."

Detective Emery looked to Mr. Dewey who stood in the corner of the room. Mr. Dewey stepped forward and said, "we'd like to search your apartment." "For what? And where's your warrant?" Samuel asked. Tobias noticed Samuel's body and face was becoming tense. "My warrant is here" Mr. Dewey said, raising a piece of paper. In a matter of minutes, Tobias along with detectives Jason Emery and another by the name Inspector Torin got in a trap with Samuel Armando.

Tobias heard the crack of the whip when the driver whipped the horse. The horse's hooves clapped against the pavement as the trap took off. Tobias was uneasy as he sat in such proximity to Detective Emery. He was hoping along the ride that he wouldn't recognize him. He didn't want to imagine what would happen if it came to that. The trap rode along bumps and rising points on the roads. Tobias kept his face turned to the small window to avoid being recognized.

The trap slowed down at certain points during the ride when the road was crowded in some areas. It then sped up once again when the road emptied. At last, the driver whipped his horse to a stop. Everyone got out one by one and Detective Emery paid the driver. Samuel led the officials with the exception of Tobias into his apartment. They had to go up four staircases to get to his apartment.

Samuel knocked at the front door. A moment later Dolores opened it. "Sam- why is the police at my door?" Dolores asked.

"They want to do a search around the apartment" Samuel said. "Why? Do you guys believe we are hiding or smuggling something illegal?" Dolores asked with rising fiery.

"Ma'am, we only wish to do a quick inspection" Detective Emery said. Dolores thought for a moment before moving aside to let them in. "I don't know what you guys think you are going to find, but you are wasting your time" she said.

In entering the apartment, the first room they saw was the kitchen. Detective Emery ordered Dolores and Samuel to stand ahead and keep out of the way. Tobias glanced at them to see what their current expression was. Dolores seemed annoyed while Samuel appeared on edge and was watching the police with a close eye.

They inspected the kitchen but found nothing out of the ordinary.

So, they moved to the bedroom with the same results and then the bathroom. Detective Emery looked around and then started for the living room with Inspector Torin. However, Tobias didn't follow. Something odd about the mirror above the sink caught his eye. When he took a closer look at the sides, he noticed that the mirror wasn't fully intact into the wall how it should be.

He messed with it a little before discovering that it could open. Tobias's eyes widened when he saw what was hiding behind the mirror. It was an air gun. He took the weapon from the shelf and went to the living room instantly.

"Mr. Emery, you should see what I found" Tobias said. Everyone in the living room turned to Tobias and he revealed what he was holding behind his back. Dolores gasped in utter shock, Samuel stumbled back in terror, and the detectives looked in amazement.

Tobias handed the air gun over to Detective Emery. "Where did you find this?" he asked.

"Behind the bathroom mirror." "I'd like to know what in the universe is an air gun doing in your house, Mr. Armando."

Dolores just stared in shock at the gun. "I...I was safe keeping it for a friend" he stammered. "You're lying!" Dolores shouted once she recovered from her shock. "Speak the truth! Why didn't you tell me there was a gun in the house? What were you planning on doing it with it?"

"I told you I was safe keeping it for a friend" Samuel said in distress. "What friend? Who are you associating yourself with?"

Tobias and the detectives stood by watching the heated couple. "I can't tell you" Samuel said. "You are going to tell me. Why aren't you able to tell me anything? You don't tell me which state you travel to see your family. And now you can't tell me who are you dealing with. This is not fair. I'm your wife and I should know what you are doing."

"Enough!" Detective Emery raised his voice. "Mr. Armando, you don't have to tell your wife anything, but you have to tell me everything. What is the purpose of an air gun in your house? Why doesn't your wife know about it? And why are you owning a gun that only government officials can own?"

Samuel sucked in a deep breath and collected himself before speaking. "I came from a village in Puerto Rico. It was a secluded village that had no kind of ruler or government, so rules were established by elders. But the rules weren't set strong and so the people did what they liked. I was young and foolish at the time. I was part of a Puerto Rican gang who committed theft and murder. The gang leader was in touch with an American gang leader because of deals and they would smuggle all kinds of weapons into Puerto Rico.

That's how this air gun came into my possession. When I was older, I met Dolores. After meeting her, I decided that I didn't want to be apart of this gang any longer.

I wanted to marry her and make a family of my own. So, together we left Puerto Rico across the borders and into America. I never told her who I really was because I saw no benefit. I took the gun with me for safety purposes because I knew the gang would come looking for me.

I don't have enough money to buy a gun and the license. This weapon is my only defense."

After Samuel told his story, the living room was silent. Tobias thought over his story and suddenly something hit him. "You say you left Puerto Rico with only Dolores?" he asked. "Yes" Samuel replied nervously. "Which means that you have no family in American and that leads to the fact that you aren't visiting family every six months."

Samuel was frozen. His mind was blank of words. He stared around helplessly. "Torin, go get a warrant for arrest and bring policemen" Detective Emery said. "Yes sir" Inspector Torin said. When Torin left, Detective Emery pulled out a pistol from his pocket. "Sit down," he said. "Good. Don't move until the police come for you." Samuel sat down as he was told. Suddenly, a wicked smile formed across his lips. Before Detective Emery could react to the sudden change of expression, Samuel pulled out a pistol from his pocket and fired at Emery.

Detective Emery's body fell instantly to the floor. Dolores screamed in horror at her husband's action. Tobias was terrified but he ran over to Detective Emery. "Don't let him go" Emery said. Tobias saw that the detective was bleeding somewhere around his chest. "Get the doctor for him," Tobias told Dolores who looked about to faint. "Can I borrow your gun? I forgot mines."

Detective Emery weakly handed the gun over to Tobias. Tobias slipped it in his pocket and started out of the apartment. Samuel had gone way before. What did I get myself into? Tobias thought. He certainly didn't think his plan of disguise would come to this. He didn't think he would have to pursue someone who was potentially dangerous and might even have to use a gun. Tobias just hoped inside it wouldn't get ugly.

16

CHAPTER 16

Tobias dodged and ducked the crowds of people while trying not to lose Samuel's head among the crowd. It was difficult moving forward through the crowd as the people didn't seem so keen on clearing a path for Tobias. He was afraid to lose his target, so he figured the only option he had was to fire the pistol.

Tobias withdrew the pistol from the pocket of his pants, raised it to the air, and pulled the trigger. The boom made him flinch and the crowd scream wildly. Samuel turned around at the gunshot to find that a path was cleared between him and his pursuer.

He broke into a run and Tobias followed closely. Every now and then Tobias fired his pistol in the air. The crowds screamed loudly and ran away instantly. Tobias's lean muscled figure gained speed quicker than the heavier built figure of Samuel. The pursuit took them through narrow roads, wide crowded streets, and many turns.

At one point, they were running toward a wagon stacked with barrels that was being drawn by a horse. Samuel fired at the wooden wheel causing it to snap.

The wagon went swaying from left to right. The horse rose on its hind legs and neighed in distress. The elderly man on the wagon tried to control the panicked horse. Barrels rolled off the wagon onto the road causing dust clouds to rise. Samuel managed to run ahead of the chaos leaving Tobias behind it.

"You will pay for this!" the old man yelled at Sameul.

Tobias couldn't afford to stand by watching Samuel's figure shrink by the moment as he got away. He needed to find a shortcut. So, he abandoned the road on which he stood on and went round to another, knowing both roads would meet. He ran swiftly along the sidewalk of the less crowded road, occasionally leaping over yard fences and dodging people.

He needed to beat Samuel to the end or else he would lose him for good. His target wasn't in the best shape for running but he was decisive and didn't stick around to see the results of his actions. On reaching the end of the road, Tobias came to a halt to catch his breath and rest his burning muscles.

He didn't see Samuel, which had him thinking that he had beaten him and was long gone. Just then he heard rapid footsteps coming forward and heavy pants. Samuel appeared at the end of the road, panting heavily. "Raise your hands!" Tobias shouted. Samuel spun around to find his pursuer pointing a gun at him.

"Or?" he asked. "I'll shoot you." "You won't because you can't. I will because I can." Samuel fired his pistol at Tobias. Tobias instantly threw himself to the ground to avoid the bullet. The bullet flew past him and into the trunk of a tree in someone's yard. Samuel aimed the pistol at Tobias to attempt a second shot but instead of looking afraid, Tobias smiled and chuckled lightly.

Confusion spread over Samuel's face causing him to withhold for a moment from pulling the trigger. Before he knew what hit him, a cane connected to his head with full force knocking him out. There stood the old man from the wagon.

"What did I say?" he said. "You will pay for what you did." Tobias rose from the ground and thanked the man. Police officers arrived in hansoms a moment later. A few went over to Samuel's figure that lay on the floor. Inspector Torin walked up to Tobias. "You did a good job catching that big guy...

"Bob Martin" Tobias gave his fake name. "Mr. Martin."

"Well, I did pursue him, but it was this old man who brought him down." Inspector Torin looked at the old man who waved his cane and he got the picture.

Samuel was brought into custody. Mr. Dewey ordered that he be locked behind bars until tomorrow when his trials in court would begin. Detective Emery was under emergency medical care for the bullet Samuel fired at him was in his lung.

Therefore, Inspector Torin and Tobias, so-called known as Bob Martin, had to lay out the story from beginning to end for Mr. Dewey. Inspector Torin's part was from when they stepped foot into the apartment to when he was sent for the police.

Tobias told the rest when Samuel shot Detective Emery and he pursued him. "And that was it" Tobias said toward the conclusion. "That's an extraordinary story," Mr. Dewey said thoughtfully. "What do you think of it all, sir?" Inspector Torin asked. "I need time to think it all over. I wish for us to meet here at 3pm tomorrow. I'll have my thoughts on everything by then."

"Good evening" Inspector Torin said as started out with Tobias. "Hey, you," Mr. Dewey called Tobias who was nearly going to close the office door. "Yes sir."

"Your face seems new around here." Tobias froze and stared at the chief nervously. "Uhh, my name is Bob Martin. I work with the lower police officers. I've been reading a lot about the murder of

Anne James and the case interests me. So, today when they brought in Samuel Armando, I decided to follow for I was curious."

Mr. Dewey looked at Tobias with interesting eyes which caused a nervousness to prickle across Tobias's skin.

"Good evening" he then said.

When Tobias returned to Greyson's house, he stuffed the beard in his pocket and then knocked at the door. The maid opened it for him. As he made way for the staircase, he found Dona sitting on the living room floor wrapping gifts. "What's the event?" he asked. "Natasha's birthday is approaching the day after tomorrow. My darling is turning twenty years old. She's going to be a young woman."

"Where is she now?" Tobias asked.

"At her friend's house."

"When will she be back?"

"Why does that matter to you?"

"I'm just curious."

"I don't know when she will be back."

"Alright, I need to apologize for the way I spoke to her on the day of the fire."

"She doesn't want your apology. She doesn't care for it or you."

Tobias stood by the staircase in silence before heading up to the bedroom. He was greeted by a massive, sleepy pooch laid out on the carpet. Bennett returned from his work as a cabman just when the moon rose above Pristine Hills, casting a white light over the forest and houses.

Dona and the cooks were bunched in the kitchen preparing supper for the household. Tobias exited the bedroom and started down the hallway when he came across the open door of Natasha's bedroom. She was standing by her gold-colored dresser trying to take off a necklace which she seemed to be having difficulty with. Tobias walked softly toward her.

Natasha saw him behind her in the mirror. "Let me help you with the necklace" he said. When she didn't say anything, he brought his hands to the silver chain and undid it for her. She took her necklace and placed it on the dresser. "I'm sorry for what I said to you on the day of the fire."

Natasha suddenly spun around with an angry glare on her normally sweet and beautiful face. "If you don't want my sympathy or sorry, I don't want yours either" she said with anger and hurt in her voice. "Natasha, you know I didn't mean what I said. You could understand that I was having a panic attack at that moment. Put yourself in my shoes. You are the heiress of this house, aren't you? What if some unknown fiend burned it down to ashes? You would be devastated, stressed, and miserable. It's not like you could do anything about it. You can't get the money for the house, let alone the house itself. I just lost half my inheritance."

Natasha's expression went from angry to sympathetic. She looked at Tobias with sympathetic green eyes.

"I'm sorry" she said. "No, I'm sorry. You didn't deserve what I said to you. You deserve more than that. Way more."

Natasha embraced her arms Tobias in a hug. Tobias returned it. "I heard your turning twenty years old." "I am. I'm excited." "Happy Early Birthday."

Natasha smiled and left a quick kiss on Tobias's cheek. "Let me finish taking my ornaments off."

17

CHAPTER 17

Tobias was eating breakfast the following morning with Brutus eating his in the corner, when Natasha walked in with a white envelope in her hands. "My father sent me a letter for birthday since he won't be here, and along with it he sent a letter for you" she said. Tobias took the envelope and withdrew the folded paper inside. He unfolded it and read the letter to himself.

Dear Tobias

I arrived yesterday in Pennsylvania during the late night. I settled in an inn and today I shall begin my investigation at your mother's family's house. How is everything with you? Has anything out of the ordinary occurred? I hope you aren't getting yourself in crazy situation or trouble.

From Dwight Greyson

"Can I have something to write with?" Tobias asked. "I brought a fountain pen. Here" Natasha said.

Tobias's response to Detective Greyson's letter went like this.

Dear Mr. Greyson

I'm glad you are settling well. I'm eager to hear how the investigation goes. I'm doing fine. Today the paper published quite the news. Samuel Armando returned from his three-week journey. The police brought him in for questioning. He resisted with strength when the police asked him where he travels to. They then said they would search his apartment. Detective Emery found an air gun behind the mirror in the bathroom. It appeared that Dolores knew nothing of the gun, because at the sight of it, she was horrified.

Samuel came with the excuse that he was safe keeping it for a friend. His wife demanded that he tell her who he was associating himself with. Detective Emery told Samuel to tell him the truth. So, Samuel gave this story of when he was young in Puerto Rico. He said he was part of a gang that committed crime and the gang leader was in touch with an American gang leader based off deals. The American criminal gang would smuggle in weapons across the border and one of them happened to be an air gun.

Samuel met Dolores during that time and decided that he wanted to marry her. So, he took his weapon, the air gun, and left the country with Dolores.

Inspector Torin who was with Detective Emery, asked Samuel if he left with family. He said no. Torin pointed out that Samuel was lying about visiting family every six months. Inspector Torin was sent for the police and an arrest warrant. Detective Emery told Samuel to sit down while they waited for the warrant and police. Samuel pulled out a pistol and shot Emery in the lung.

Samuel ran out of his apartment and another police officer who was there had to pursue him. The result was the police officer capturing his prisoner and the police arriving. Samuel is now in custody. I don't know what they plan on doing with him.

From Tobias James

Tobias folded the paper and put it in a brand-new envelope which Natasha brought him. "I'll take this to post office myself being that

I'm heading out later" he said. "Where are you going to later?" Natasha asked. "I need to take care of some business and pick out some gifts for you. Why?"

"My college program gives me off, so I wanted to spend time with you." Tobias found it difficult to reject Natasha, but he had a busy day ahead after breakfast. "I wish I had time to spare for you, but I don't and I'm sorry. I promise to you give time tomorrow and the day after."

"I understand," Natasha said. "It's okay." After Tobias cleared his plate, he went upstairs to get dressed in his professional attire which was a suit, a knee-lengthened coat, and brimmed hat. He put the fake beard in his pocket and started out. He flagged a hansom from the road and ordered the driver to take him to the bank. When he arrived at the bank, he found the officer to whom his father gave the gold and opal to for safe keeping. He knew it was the man for he asked his father last night who he handed the gold over to.

Tobias asked the man for a small piece of his gold. When he got it, he secured it in his pocket and took another hansom to the jewel street where shops sold gold, silver, diamonds, and more. It was a good two hours of checking in every shop to try and sell the tiny piece of gold. At one point, Tobias sat on a bench feeling like it was hopeless in trying to sell the tiny piece of gold. No one wanted to buy it because it was expensive being that it was real gold. But he reminded himself why he was trying to do sell it and so he rose with determination.

At last, he entered a shop and advertised his gold to the man behind the counter. The man seemed interested and bought the gold at the price given. Tobias left the shop with the money feeling thankful and happy. He reversed his steps to the start of the jewel street where he began and went into a shop that sold a variety of rings.

Tobias took his time looking through the display glass of rings. His eyes went through the gold rings, the silver rings, emerald rings, and finally diamond rings. A ring made of silver with a diamond on it caught his attention. "Perfect" he said.

"Can I have this one, sir?" he asked the man who was sitting in a chair. The man rose from his seat and walked around the counter to where Tobias stood. "Which one?" he asked.

"That one," Tobias pointed. "I'm guessing this is for a proposal" the man said, taking the ring from its slot. "A proposal which I nervous to death about" Tobias said. "I'll give you one piece of advice," the man said. "The only way to find out what the answer will be is to propose." "I won't forget that. I would like for the ring to be in a velvet wedding ring box."

After getting the wedding ring and paying for it with the money he got from the gold, Tobias took a hansom to a flower shop where he purchased a bouquet of pink and white peonies. He then went to a sweet shop and picked out a box of chocolates. The last thing he bought was birthday cards with messages in them. Tobias put the gifts in a bag to conceal them from Natasha's sight.

When he knocked at the front door, it was she who opened it. "You're back early" she said. "I have a meeting in thirty minutes," Tobias said. "I will be heading out again.

Is there anywhere in the house where I can put these things? Somewhere no one will find them." "You can put them in my closet. I'm the only one who goes in it." Tobias followed Natasha to the staircase. From corner of the kitchen doorway, Dona peeked at the two as they headed upstairs. Her eyes landed on the bag in Tobias's hand. "I think I will put it on top of the closet. Promise me you won't touch anything or even take a glance." "You can trust me, Toby."

Tobias placed a chair near the closet and stood on it. He placed the bag carefully atop and then stepped down. "When will you be back?" Natasha asked. "I'll be back when I'm back," he said, smiling warmly at her. "Don't you worry. And please look after Brutus for me."

When Tobias left the house, he put a distance between him and it before putting on his fake beard. He then waved down a hansom from the street and took it to the DPA department. On entering, he started for the staircase to the second floor where he found Mr. Dewey's office room. He knocked at the door. "Come in" said Mr. Dewey. Tobias opened the door and stepped in the room. Inspector Torin had already seated himself in one of the two chairs by Mr. Dewey's desk.

"Good evening," Mr. Dewey said. "Take a seat."

Tobias sat down nervously. He didn't know what to except from Mr. Dewey, and that was making him uneasy.

"I thought about Samuel Armando and the case since yesterday until today, and I've formed a final opinion with the help of Torin." "Torin?" Tobias said questioningly.

"Yes, he's my son." Tobias gave a surprised start.

"Are you serious?"

"I'm serious. We spoke to Detective Emery about our opinion being that he is a very experienced detective. Not that I need his advise because I'm the chief, but it's always good to hear other's opinions. He didn't say much for he was weak and could barely speak due to his punctured lung, but he agreed that it all made sense. Samuel's court trials started this morning, by the way.

Here's what we all agreed on. Dolores Armando, Wendy Hudson, and Ted Wilson are guilty of the murder of Anne James."

Tobias froze in his seat, staring at Mr. Dewey in disbelief. "We have proof and facts to support this. The scheme started five years ago when Wendy apologized to her husband and faked to love him. She did this so it wouldn't appear that she committed the murder over jealousy. She would be able to tell anyone that she loves her husband and doesn't care about Bennett James any longer. Being that her and Dolores are close friends, she pulled her into the scheme with money as the bait. Everyone knows the Armandos are poor.

They needed someone to do the shooting, someone who had the skill. Dolores suggested Mr. Wilson. We don't know the situation between those two, but we do know is that there is some sort of friendly relationship there. Dolores said she would lend her husband's air gun to Mr. Wilson being that it is silent when fired-

"Excuse me, sir. Why was she horrified when we found it?" Tobias asked.

"Because that was the weapon they used to murder Anne. She was horrified that we would connect the facts of the case and she would be among the guilty suspects. Now let's come to the day of the murder. Wendy and Mr. Wilson met in Dolores's apartment while Anne was at work. What supports this is that both of them lied of where they were on that morning. One doesn't lie if they don't fear the truth. Wendy laid out her plan to them and then went on her way. Dolores gave the air gun to Mr. Wilson, and he positioned himself in the abandoned apartment building down the street. We learned that could've been the only perching place where the alleyway is visible from.

Dolores soaked a couple of clothes in water, put them in a laundry basket, and went over to the window to start hanging them. Anne exited the building and Dolores called her out.

She bought Mr. Wilson time to aim and shoot by exchanging friendly words with her. If you think it over, the facts fit in well and it sounds reasonable."

"What about the men in the woods? Who burned Tobias's house? Who followed him and his father? Who tried to kidnap Tobias? And what is Samuel doing when he leaves the neighborhood every six months?"

"That is another case which Dwight Greyson is dealing with. It's no doubt that Anne had enemies that are now after her family. Samuel's case is useless to investigate. He's in custody and will be tried in court. If he doesn't want to say anything about what he was doing, it doesn't matter for he will received a sentence of prison."

Tobias was left speechless. He didn't have anything to say against what the police already confirmed. "Well, what do you think?" Mr. Dewey asked. "It all fits in well, sir" Tobias said.

"I thought so," Mr. Dewey said. "The case is officially closed and will be announced so in a few days."

"Aren't you going to arrest the guilty suspects?"

"We have already. Earlier this morning."

When Tobias stepped out of the department, he wasn't sure if he should return to the house or go to the woods. He decided that going to the house wasn't a good idea for him and those in the house. If he returned home, he might have an outrageous burst if someone tried to speak to him.

He definitely didn't want to say anything hurtful to Natasha. That would hurt his chances of receiving a yes for his proposal. So, he turned in the direction of the forest.

The road eventually faded into a forest trail when he neared the woods. Tobias wondered off the trail and into the trees and vegetation. His ears picked up the sound of the bubbling stream which he used to guide him to it. After walking through leaves, twigs, and trees, Tobias arrived at his go-to area when he was stress or needed a piece of mind.

He sat on the log and stared ahead at the stream. "Everything that Mr. Dewey explained made sense," he said. "But why do I feel like it isn't right? Like it was someone else who murdered my mom and not them? Those unordinary events which I witnessed took place after her murder. The men in the woods, the attempted kidnapping on me, the mystery follower, and the burning of my house. If these events occurred because of the enemy or enemies of my mom, why did they rise after she was killed? And why was she killed the day after telling me of my inheritance? Was that a coincidence or did someone know?"

With so many questions running through Tobias's mind, he was beginning to grow frustrated, and his inside was becoming hot with anger. "I can't let this case go," he said, rising and pacing up and down in an anxious manner. "This case is not over! I don't care what the police think or say! The killer is still out there!

And I will find him. If he thinks he can rest assured that the police closed the case, he is thinking wrong because what he doesn't know is that I will catch him sooner or later. But if I do that, what will I do when I find him? If I bring him and truth of the case to the police, they will kill me for performing an illegal and unofficial investigation.

Hold on, why am I afraid now to die? This is not how I thought in the beginning. I didn't care about my life because it had no purpose but now...it does. That's Natasha.

Why was I given a purpose now? Why?"

Tobias kicked his leg into the trunk of a tree. "If I bring the truth to the police, my life will be jeopardized, and I'll have no chance of ever being with Natasha!"

The anger and fury boiling up in Tobias's heart felt like physical heat. To him, all this would've never happened if it wasn't for the killer of his mother. "Whoever you are, I swear that I will kill you when I find you! No one will stop me! Not the police, not the government, and not the law!"

An hour later found Tobias riding in a hansom back to the house. When the hansom pulled up, he paid the driver and went up to the front door before knocking at it.

The maid opened the door and Tobias walked in.

As he went into the kitchen for a glass of water, he found Natasha placing Brutus's bowl down with his lunch. Tobias took a glass from the cupboard and filled it with water from a bottle in the refrigerator. "How was your day outside?" Natasha asked.

"Tobias, get over here right now!" Dona's angry voice suddenly broke in. "You as well, Natasha!" "Mom? What happened?" Natasha asked. "Follow me, the two of you, to your bedroom!"

18

———— ❖ ————

CHAPTER 18

Dona marched upstairs with Tobias and Natasha following, both lost at what triggered this sudden anger in her. She brought them to Natasha's bedroom and slammed the door shut. "Tell me what in the universe is all this!" Dona said, grabbing Tobias's bag which was on Natasha's bed and dumping everything out of it.

Everything inside it was scattered on the floor. The bouquet of peonies, the box of chocolates, the birthday cards, and the wedding ring box. Natasha stared at the items in utter shock. Tobias was just as shocked, but at the fact that Dona somehow discovered the stuff. His shock however transformed into anger. "How dare you?" he raised his voice. "What is wrong with you? Dumping my stuff on the floor like its trash! Do you have shame?"

"What did you think you were doing? Were you going to ask my daughter in marriage behind her parents' backs?"

"No, I have shame unlike you! I was going to send a letter to her father before asking!"

"Do you think Dwight is going to let you marry our daughter? You're a lunatic! We all saw you burst in rage on the day of the fire and say hurtful things to my darling! You even got yourself into trouble with the police! Do you seriously think that Dwight will grant you approval? I don't think so!"

"He apologized to me," Natasha spoke up. "He's not what you think he is!"

"I don't want to hear it, Natasha," Dona said. "Tobias is not the right one for you. I can see him dragging you into trouble in the future-

"Shut your mouth!" Tobias yelled. "Stay out of my business, you shameless woman! How dare you throw my stuff on the floor like that? Do you know what I did to buy that ring? I took a piece of my gold, went around for two hours trying to sell it, got the money at last, and finally picked out the best diamond ring that was there. What happens between me and Natasha is none of your business! I will get her father's approval and you will not interfere in my business anymore! Pick up my stuff and put it in the bag!"

Tobias's rage seemed to have a masterful effect over Dona, because she said nothing but picked up his stuff and put it in the bag. Tobias snatched his bag from Dona, flung the door open, and left the room to his.

Natasha and her mother heard his door slam close. "You are a shame, mother" Natasha said, starting out of the bedroom. "I was protecting my little girl" Dona said. "I'm not a little girl."

Natasha walked down the hallway but stopped in her steps when she heard Tobias yell in his bedroom, "I can't do this any longer!" She sighed with sympathy, wishing she could do something to help him.

The night found Tobias laying in his mattress in pajamas with Brutus beside him on the carpet. He skipped lunch and dinner due to lack of appetite. The bedroom door opened slowly and Bennett walked in with an oil lamp his hand. Tobias took no notice of him.

Bennett placed the lamp on a small table between the mattresses. "How was your day?" he asked. "Great" Tobias replied. "Dona told me of what happened earlier." "And what are you going to tell me? Throw out the stuff?"

"No, that's not what I'm going to tell you. I approve of your choice and I think it would be best to ask Mr. Greyson when he returns. These kinds of matters are best discussed face to face."

"I thought the same."

"Something seems to be bothering you."

"I'm just irritated with Mrs. Greyson. I'm not a fan of her characteristic. Throwing my stuff on the floor, exposing my proposal to Natasha, she's very annoying. I didn't plan for the proposal to happen like that. I wonder what Natasha thinks about it all."

"When Dona was telling me of what happened, Natasha defended you and spoke high of you. I'm sure your chances of receiving a positive answer are high. I know the both of you will be a successful couple. She's got wealth and so do you. With wealth, education, and morals, I know the both of you will achieve great things."

"Those things are important when marriage is considered, but without love, respect, and honor, there is no success and achievements."

"You're right. I think I'm going to hit the sac now. I had a long day of work."

"Get up, sleepy head" said a voice. Tobias blinked the sleep from his eyes and stretched out. He found Natasha sitting by his bed. "I brought you breakfast because you haven't eaten since yesterday afternoon," she said. "Drink water first."

Tobias sat up, took the glass of water, and sipped it down. "Thank you" he said. "It's okay." Natasha gave him the plate of toast and two boiled eggs. Tobias ate his breakfast fast and heartily as if he hadn't eaten in ages. He returned the plate to the tray and took the cup of green tea.

"I'm sorry about yesterday" Natasha said. "No, you're mother should be sorry for treating my stuff like garbage and spoiling my proposal" Tobias said, trying to keep his tone calm and steady. He could feel the anger from yesterday creeping to his heart. Natasha looked at him with sympathy in her green eyes. Tobias stared at his tea. "I feel embarrassed," he said lowly, staring at the smoke dance up from the hot beverage. "I feel ruined and humiliated."

Natasha took up his free hand and Tobias raised his head to look at her. "You need not feel embarrassed, ruined, or humiliated," she said softly. "Because I accept your proposal." Tobias was taken aback by shock, joyous shock though. "Whatever happens or whatever anyone says, I promise from this day till my last day that I'm yours." "And I promise the same" Tobias said, with emotion and joy in his voice.

From that moment, Tobias realized that he couldn't afford to jeopardize his life. But at the same time, he made a promise to avenge his mother and he wasn't going to break it for anything. So, he realized that there was a way to have both Natasha and his revenge.

19

CHAPTER 19

Tobias couldn't remember the last time he felt happy or even enjoyed a day of his life since his mother was killed. Yesterday was that day where he felt a sense of happiness and joy. After Natasha accepted his proposal in the morning, he gave her the gifts which he bought, the bouquet of peonies, the box of sweets, and the birthday cards. They decided that the ring would be saved for their wedding day when they were actually married.

The approaching evening brought Natasha's friends to the house along with plenty of birthday presents. Dona and the cooks presented the birthday cake which they had been working on since yesterday. It was a vanilla and strawberry flavored cake, loaded with butter frosting, and decorated with strawberry slices.

The cake had two layers, so the top had candles stuck in it. Everyone sang to Natasha while she stood there shyly, before blowing the candles out. Everyone enjoyed a slice of cake and a glass of refreshing fruit punch. The party extended until the late evening. Natasha and her friends as well as Tobias told jokes, exchanged long conversations, had more cake and fruit punch, and danced.

The day after the birthday, Tobias took Natasha to eat at a diner. After lunch, they bought tickets for the theatre. When the play finished, they went to Paradise Beverage Bar for smoothies and then home. Dona wasn't very happy about Tobias taking her daughter out, but little did she know that they were engaged to be married. Tobias asked Natasha what her mother's problem was, and she explained that her mother wanted her to be her little girl forever. She didn't want her to grow up although her daughter already grew up.

The following day, Tobias was reading the Pristine Magazine on an armchair in the living room. Today's news announced that the Pristine Hills Murder was officially closed. Dolores Armando, Wendy Hudson, and Ted Wilson were sentenced with a certain number of years to prison. The paper said that in the last trial at court, the guilty suspects finally admitted with their own lips that everything the police put together was true, and that they were guilty of the murder of Anne James.

Tobias couldn't bear to read another word of what he thought was a lie, and so he threw the paper into the fire. He stared angrily into the flames. The flaring flames reflected the heat rising in his heart. He didn't care what anyone said. In his opinion, the police were lying about the suspects claiming guilty. "Toby, my father sent a letter for you" came the voice of Natasha.

Tobias turned his head to find Natasha standing beside him with an envelope in her hand. He took the envelope and withdrew the letter from inside. The letter read:

Dear Tobias

I thought my investigation at Pennsylvania would take two weeks, but it turns out I'm returning today. I got what I expected from this investigation. The butler your mother told you about who attempted to steal her mother's gold was actually a man by the name

Micheal Sebastian. Sebastian and Anne were engaged to be married many years ago before she ever left and married your father. Her parents, Olivia and Patrick learned that Sebastian's intentions of marrying their daughter was for her wealth which she would inherit. So, they cut the engagement quickly. Sebastian became angry and fought with the parents, but it was clear that he wasn't getting his way. He disappeared for a year before returning as a butler under the disguise of Oliver Hunt.

He worked full time at Anne's family's house, and soon learned where the gold was being kept. His attempt was a failure and he was sentenced to prison. When he was released, he fled and was never seen again. I believe he has returned for his revenge.

From Dwight Greyson

Tobias took up a fountain pen from mantlepiece and began writing his reply to the letter.

Dear Mr. Greyson

What you say makes sense. I feel that my mother was anxious the day she told me of my inheritance because she knew Sebastian had returned. Perhaps she saw him when she went out or he left her a sign of his presence.

The police over here closed the case. They confirmed that the suspects are Wendy Hudson, Dolores Armando, and Ted Wilson. It was also discovered that Samuel Armando was getting paid to get immigrants over the borders from North America and the Caribbeans. So, they have all been sentenced with years of prison. The paper mentioned that they with the exception of Samuel claimed to be guilty of the murder.

Anyway, I have my reasons for believing that they got the suspects wrong and the case isn't over even if they say so.

From Tobias James

Tobias took his letter to the post office. When he returned, he went upstairs to his bedroom. He rummaged through his clothes in the closet and found the record of the case which he had been updating since it started.

He sat in his mattress with Brutus beside him and started reading over the case from its very first developments till the current ones. As he revised the record, he began to notice that the story the police confirmed to be true was false. One would have to look into the depths of the story to find the hints that gave away its falsehood, and that's what Tobias did.

In the first place, Wendy didn't plan to murder Anne. Who in their right mind would decide to plan a murder fifteen years later and then wait five years to put it into action?

In the second place, why would Wendy go to Dolores's house along with Mr. Butcher to lay out her plan and their roles on the very day of the murder? Anyone planning for a murder lays out the roles and plans days before it occurs.

In the third place, there is no connection between Dolores and Mr. Butcher. The day they spoke at Paradise Beverage Bar was the first time they had ever met one another. Tobias decided on this for when they were sitting side by side, they said nothing for some moments. If they knew each other, they would start talking instantly.

In the fourth place, Dolores never knew her husband had an air gun behind the bathroom mirror. Nor was it in the house when the murder occurred because he was away at the borders by South America.

That meant he had the gun with him. After realizing these facts which didn't support the polices' story, Tobias concluded that the story was completely false and so were the suspects.

He also knew that the police were aware, because if he, an unofficially without training, can spot these facts in the story, the police could in an instant. "Brutus, the police are hiding something," Tobias told his dog. "That killer is still out there and the police know. I desperately need to discuss this with Mr. Greyson. I'm sure he will agree with me."

20

CHAPTER 20

During the midnight, Detective Greyson returned from Pennsylvania. The following morning at breakfast, Bennett told him that he was going to move out by tomorrow being that the case was closed.

Tobias and Detective Greyson met in the living room after breakfast. Tobias explained the story the police stated to be true. Detective Greyson listened carefully. When Tobias concluded the story, Detective Greyson instantly pointed out the facts that went against the story. Surprisingly, they were the exact same facts Tobias thought of yesterday.

So, he mentioned to Greyson that he thought the same and that he felt the police were hiding something they were guilty of. Detective Greyson agreed with him, but when Tobias asked if he was going to act, he replied that he couldn't for several reasons.

Acting against the police would mean destroying his life, himself, his family, his title, and just about everything. Tobias knew he couldn't tell his plan to Greyson, but he didn't care because he was still going to do it. After discussing that part of what Tobias wanted to speak out, he brought up his proposal to Natasha and what happened with Dona.

Detective Greyson wasn't very surprised by the news. He said he saw it coming by the interactions between Tobias and his daughter. Greyson gave Tobias permission to marry his daughter, but with one condition. He would have to wait until Natasha graduated from college, because he didn't want the burden of marriage and eventually children on her shoulders while still attending college. Tobias didn't care how long he had to wait, as long as he knew Natasha was his.

When night fell upon Pristine Hills and Bennett returned from work, Detective Greyson said, "Mr. James, do you know about your son's proposal to my daughter?"

"Yes, he told me." "Great. Tobias just told me of it earlier and I wasn't surprised as I was expecting it. I gave him permission to take Natasha's hand in marriage- "Really, father?" Natasha exclaimed in surprisement.

"Of course, my darling." "Thank you, father. Thank you. I was afraid you wouldn't allow it." "Why should I hold my daughter back from marrying a good man like Tobias? But you must graduate from college before any marriage takes place."

"Of course, father." "I was wondering if you would agree, Mr. James." "Why should I not? They're the perfect match. Both are young, wealthy, educated, and smart. I can see them achieving great things together."

"I agree with you, Mr. James. Their love and respect toward one another are part of achieving great things in a marriage as well."

That's odd. He's the second person after me to say that to my father Tobias thought.

"I'm glad we both agreed" Detective Greyson said. "Has everyone forgot that I'm one of the parents as well?" Dona asked. "No one has asked me if I agree to this."

"Dona, it's already agreed to. Your disagreement will not break the agreement. The only reason you are preventing Natasha from getting married is because you don't want her to grow up. You must fight that feeling."

"That's not fair!" Dona cried. "She's my daughter and should be allowed to make decisions when regarding to her!" Dona slapped the dining table and stomped out of the dining room angrily. Everyone exchanged an amused expression.

After dinner was cleared from the table, Tobias and Bennett went upstairs to their bedroom. "I found a small apartment for us to move into tomorrow," Bennett said. "We will have to bear with the limited space, but I'm working to get something bigger." "It's not a problem."

The golden rays of the dawn sun were a pleasant sight to Tobias. The light gave him this sense of hope and success with his life. But he wished that it didn't have to take his mother being killed for him to meet Natasha. He wished his mother could have met Natasha and been there to see how he progressed in life. One thing he did learn was that no matter what happened, no matter how hopeless the situation appeared, it would end and ease would come.

Tobias took up his watch from the side table and looked at the message engraved it behind it. I love you to the moon and back ~ Mom. "I love you, mom. I wish you were here with me."

He put his watch on and got out of bed to start his day. Today, he and his father would be moving out.

"Morning, sunshine" Tobias told Natasha, seating himself beside her at the breakfast along with his father and Dona. He gave her a quick kiss on the cheek. "Morning, how did you sleep?" Natasha asked. "Good. Isn't your father going to join us at breakfast?"

"He's visiting Mr. Emery at the hospital" Dona said, staring at Tobias in disgust at the sweet name calling and the kiss on the cheek.

Everyone dug into breakfast hungrily and then Tobias and his father started packing their stuff for the move. Detective Greyson returned by lunch time but he looked grief-stricken. He picked at his food with lack of appetite. "Why aren't you eating, darling?" Dona asked her husband, taking his hand.

"Jason passed away," he said. Everyone at the dining table froze. "He was my best friend and mentor when I joined the force as an inexperienced detective. He was an amazing, strong, and intelligent man who brought this neighborhood justice throughout his years of serving as a detective. I shall never forget him."

Everyone shared a long moment of silent grief, but no one was more grief stricken than Greyson.

"What do you plan on doing today?" Bennett said, after having breakfast for the first time in their small apartment. "I might visit Natasha," Tobias replied. "When will you be able to pay for my college?" "I'm working on it. You'll recontinue going very soon. But you must understand that I'm trying to pay the rent for this apartment along with groceries, your dog's meat, the horse's food, and soon your college again."

"I understand, but I don't see how you've been unable to pay for my college when you have been paying for it since I attended."

"Like I said, when your mother was killed, it became harder for me. She helped me with the financial situation and that made it easier."

"Mom worked only three days a week, and her job was low paying. The money she earned was used for groceries. I understand that you started paying for groceries after she was killed, but I'm wondering where the rest of your earning went to."

"Put yourself in my shoes and then come question my work."

Bennett put his hat on, exited the front door, and slammed it shut.

"You want to go for a walk, Brutus?" Tobias asked the dog who was sitting by. Brutus stood up, wagging his tail excitedly at the hearing of going out. "Come on, let's get ready."

21

⸺ ◆ ⸺

CHAPTER 21

"You look beautiful" Tobias said, as Natasha exited her house. Tobias was taking her out for dinner at the well-known diner known as Comfort Zone, which is owned by Detective Greyson. Natasha was wearing a sky blue dress with elegant feathers and hat with a bow. Her face was decorated with pink lipstick, blush, eye shadow, and eyeliner. In her arm she held her handbag.

"Thank you," she said, smiling shyly. "You look amazing as well." She slipped her arm through Tobias's and together they walked to the trap which awaited them by the side of the pavement. Tobias let her get in first before following.

The ride was smooth and quick to Comfort Zone. Tobias and Natasha stepped out and paid the driver. They walked arm in arm into the diner. Comfort Zone wasn't like the ordinary packed diners that were stuffy, crowded, and everyone was bunched together.

As a matter of a fact, it was a hotspot for adults who wanted a breather from their children. The glossy wooden tables and cushioned chairs were spaced out from one another, giving the diners privacy. This also helped avoid stuffiness.

Young couples, parents, friends, and elderly couples were only types of diners seen. "The table over there is empty" Natasha said, looking to an empty table on the left. She and Tobias walked over to it and seated themselves on the chairs.

"What do you think?" Natasha asked. "This is your first time being here." "It's a fine diner," Tobias replied. "Your father had a good idea when he invested to build this place."

Tobias and Natasha studied the menu, before a waiter came over to them with his clipboard and pencil. "What can I get for you two?" he asked. "Can I have the salmon with gravy and asparagus please?" Natasha asked. The waiter scribbled down the order and then looked to Tobias. "I'll have the lobster tail with mashed potatoes and string beans." The waiter wrote down the order. "Anything else?" "Perhaps two pineapple juices" Natasha said.

The waiter was on his way to deliver their order to the kitchen. "You haven't said anything since the police found the killers and sentenced them to prison. Why is that?" Natasha asked. The question took Tobias by surprise. It was only between him and Detective Greyson that the police got the suspects wrong, and they knew it.

"Are you going to tell me what's going on?" Natasha asked, as if sensing that there was something going on behind the scenes.

"I will tell you but you can't mention it to anyone. Only your father and I are aware. Everyone else thinks this is true. Everything the police said in that paper was false. They arrested innocent people, the story they told was false, and they are aware of their actions."

"Are you serious?"

"I'm serious. That's why I haven't said anything about the news. I'm not happy nor satisfied with it."

"What are you going to do about it?"

"What can I do? I'm an unofficial. If I try to do something, I will jeopardize my life forever. I've already been warned by the police, actually the chief himself."

The waiter arrived in the middle of their conversation with a tray of two plates and two glasses. He begun laying their food and juice infront of them. From the corner of his eye, Tobias spotted two men entering the diner. Something about their appearance caught his attention. One had a short black beard and the other had a grey mustache.

Tobias's heart literally leaped out of his chest when he recognized the men to be those from the woods. The waiter finished laying the food out and he was on his way. Tobias avoided directly staring at the men for he didn't want them to spot him. So, he side eyed them while trying to eat his food at the same time.

Natasha noticed his manner quickly. "Who are you looking at?" she asked. "Those men" Tobias said. Natasha looked to where he was looking and saw them taking a table. "I don't see what's so interesting about two ordinary men coming for dinner."

"They are no ordinary men. I saw these men in the woods and they have something to do with my mother's murder. Don't look at them directly. I don't want them to notice."

Tobias watched at the men spoke in proximity before a waiter walked up to them. They told the waiter what they wanted and he went off to the kitchen. The men seemed to be acting cautious, for they glanced around here and there. They also spoke in proximity while keeping their voices low.

Tobias didn't remove his eyes from them for one second. The man with the beard took another glance at their surroundings, but this time his eyes met those of Tobias. Something about the man's eyes were oddly familiar to Tobias. This nerve-racking familiarity about the man's eyes prickled at Tobias's heart.

22

CHAPTER 22

r. Beard said something to Mr. Mustache and the men got up from their seats. They started out of the diner. "I'm sorry, Natasha. I can't let these men go" Tobias said, shoving aside his chair and starting for the doorway. "I will tell my father" Natasha said.

When Tobias and Natasha exited the diner, Natasha went a separate way in the direction of her house to inform her father. Tobias spotted the men getting into a trap that was attached to a grey horse. When Mr. Beard whipped the horse to start running, Tobias knew he needed to pursue them. This was his chance to recover the truth that he had been seeking for.

So, when he spotted a man riding down the road on a hansom, he jumped onto the street and waved his arms. The man whipped his horse to a halt. "Give me your hansom! I need it!" Tobias said loudly. "Are you okay?" the man asked. Tobias looked ahead to see the trap getting away. "It's urgent. I'll pay you a hundred dollars if you let me burrow it."

"Sure, take it" the man said, his face lighting up like the sun at the hearing of money. Tobias got onto the hansom and whipped the horse. The brown stallion neighed and took off down the road. Mr.

Mustache turned his head around to find a pursuer on their back. Tobias could see him say something to Mr. Beard and Mr. Beard commanded the horse to run faster.

As their trap picked up speed, so did Tobias's hansom. Being that his vehicle was light and small, he caught up to them pretty quickly. The crowds of people walking along the pavement and road were quick to get out of the pursuit's way. No one wanted to be trampled by stampeding horses. The trap made a left turn and the hansom followed. The pursuit found its way into the market area of the neighborhood which the most crowded and packed place.

Mr. Mustache pulled out a pistol from his coat and fired two bullets into the air. The bang of the gun rung through the atmosphere causing both merchants and shoppers to scream and run. The trap recklessly crashed through crates of fruits and vegetables, food carts, and mini stands. Tobias found himself falling behind as watermelons, bananas, tomatoes, and squash came rolling his way.

He saw the trap growing smaller for the distance between him and it stretched. He whipped the horse harder so it could increase speed. The horse tried to run faster but the fruits and vegetables coming at its way and hitting it made it panic.

The horse accidentally stepped on a tomato which then smashed causing the horse to slip. The hansom bucked with the horse's slip and Tobias went flying off it. His body crashed into a table which was part of an outdoor cafe. He groaned at the pain in his back from the rough landing.

He watched as the horse began regaining its footing and then the trap growing smaller by the second. He rose despite the pain and walked over to the horse. Undoing the hansom which was attached to it, he got onto the saddle and grabbed the reigns.

The horse took off at high speeds after the trap. By now, the trap was nearing the end of the market area. "Run faster, boy," Tobias said. "The fastest you've ever ran. I'll give you all the apples you could dream of having."

Somehow as if understanding or feeling Tobias's words, the horse picked up speed by the second and soon it was flying with the wind. The trap arrived at the end of the market and so it turned right. Tobias's horse turned right as well and soon Tobias was on his targets' back.

Tobias spotted the train tracks ahead and so do his targets. He heard the crack of the whip as they commanded their horse to run faster. Then came the long honk of the train horn. The train was racing down the tracks. He knew he wasn't going to make it across for he was behind, but his targets had a chance.

The train's horn grew louder. The distance between the trap and the tracks cut shorter. Tobias watched while still pursuing them. His heart thumped heavily as he didn't want to see what would happen if they didn't make it across. Suddenly, before his eyes, the train flies by at blurring speeds. His targets are out of sight. When the long body of locomotive ends, he spotted them on the other side and they were getting away. "Run!" Tobias commanded the horse.

By now, his horse was in a pool of perspiration and it was breathing heavily. It ran as fast as it could, but it wasn't fast enough to keep up with the trap. "They're getting away!" Tobias cried in desperation.

Just then, a black horse with a woman riding it came out of nowhere infront of the trap. "Stop there!" the woman said. "Natasha?" Tobias said in a low and confused voice. Following her was her father on a brown horse. He held a pistol in his hand which he aimed at the men, whose trap was halted.

Tobias arrived at the scene and slowed down his horse. "Drop your weapons and raise your hands!" Detective Greyson said in a bold and loud voice. Mr. Beard descended the trap and so did Mr. Mustache. Detective Greyson jumped off his horse. Tobias and Natasha did the same. "Drop your weapons" Greyson said.

"I don't think so" Mr. Mustache said, aiming his gun at Detective Greyson. Natasha gasped fearfully. "Father, back off" she said. "It's over," Mr. Beard said in his deep voice. "Just drop the weapon."

"I'm not a quitter like you" Mr. Mustache said. "I will say it one more time. Drop your weapon" Greyson said. "What about this" and Mr. Mustache fired at Detective Greyson before breaking into a run. Natasha cried out and ran over to her father who fell to the ground. Tobias started after Mr. Mustache instantly.

The man didn't get far before Tobias caught up with him. In just a second they were engaged in a full on physical fight. Tobias picked up at the man was desperate to flee, but for some reason his partner had no intention of fleeing for he stood by where he was caught. The man threw punches at Tobias. Tobias avoided most of them with ducks and backing off, but he did get hit on the sides and face a few times.

The man grabbed Tobias by his coat and seized his tie before wrapping it around his throat. Tobias strained against the choke lock and attempted to remove his own tie from his neck. He brought his hands to the man's face and looked to target his ears.

When he got his hands on the man's ears, he pulled them hard enough for the man to screech in pain and let him go. Tobias stumbled forward gasping for oxygen. His opponent came running at him behind. With the perfect timing and aim, Tobias hurled around and threw a blow into his nose.

The man tumbled backward cupping his hands around his nose. Tears rose in his eyes and blood trickled from his nostrils. Tobias marched up to his opponent, grabbed him by the coat, and threw furious punches into his face. He spotted the gun in the man's pocket and took it. The man's eyes were tearing up in pain as his face was being hit with a recking ball of fury and anger.

His sense of judgement and alertness was out of the window. Tobias aimed the gun at him. "Walk!" he yelled. When he saw that the man was too focused on the pain he received from the punches, he grabbed him by the collar of coat and roughly walked him back to where the rest were.

Natasha was helping her father up who fortunately just shot on the shoulder. Mr. Beard remained put where he was which Tobias thought to be unordinary being that his partner was determined to escape.

Tobias shoved Mr. Mustache beside Mr. Beard. "Are you okay, Mr. Greyson?" Tobias asked. "I'm fine. Fortunately, it wasn't a fatal area he hit. Just my shoulder" Greyson said, holding his bleeding shoulder with his daughter by his side.

"Take off that fake beard and mustache" he told the men, whiling holding his gun at them. "One thing before I do it," Mr. Mustache said. "I'm not guilty of anything that I did." He rips off his mustache and there standing before Tobias is Torin Dewey, the son of Frank Dewey chief of the DPA.

"What the... Tobias just stared at the man who stood before him in utter shock. Anger was beginning was rise within him like lava before the volcano erupts. "And you?" he turned to Mr. Beard. Mr. Beard stared at Tobias for a moment before taking his fake beard off slowly.

Natasha gasped in the most utter shock at who she saw. Detective Greyson's eyes grew wide and his jaw fell. Tobias wondered how he didn't faint. "Dad?" he whispered. There stood Bennett James standing there with guilt and sadness written all over his face.

Tobias's body was starting to tremble. He felt his heart, lungs, and mind beginning to race. Flashbacks and voices flashed before his eyes.

'Where did you get that scarf from?'

He looked at the scarf as if he recognized it.

'I don't want you going to those woods often. That's where kidnappers set up their traps.'Right after he said that, just about two or three days later, a man by the name Jack Oberon tries to kidnap. He was sent to scare Tobias from woods because that was the their secret meeting area.

'Yesterday while I was at work I noticed a man who seemed to be following me on his trap.'

After that was said, Tobias spotted a man following him when he went out.

'I didn't want to tell you because I didn't want you stressing, but money is low and I can't afford to send you back for a while.'

The money was low because he was paying Torin Dewey to do these tasks for him.

'It was two days before my wedding. Mrs. James moved into the neighborhood a week before my wedding. She was a rich woman and wanted to build her dream house in Pristine Hills. She hired construction workers from the company and one of them was Mr. James.'

'Toby, I don't want you going to the woods often.'

He said that morning following when Tobias saw the two strangers in the woods. It wasn't a coincidence. It was him trying to scare Tobias away from the woods being that it was his secret meeting area.

'They're the perfect match. Both are young, wealthy, educated, and smart.'

Bennett only ever looked at wealth and education when it came to marriage. Tobias had never heard his father mention that love and respect is part of getting together. That was the answer to why Bennett changed his mind about marrying Wendy Hudson. He saw that Anne had money and education, and he was a poor construction worker who was hungry for wealth.

It all made sense now to Tobias. All this time the answers were so simple and right infront of him.

23

———— ❖ ————

CHAPTER 23

"**A**re you sick in the head?" Tobias yelled. His voice screamed out pain and anger. "Did you really kill her?" Bennett looked down in guilt. "I did." "Say you didn't!" Tobias marched up to his father, seized him by the coat, and shoved him against the wall of the bridge they stood under. "I would be lying if I said I didn't!" Bennett raised his voice slightly.

"Why did you kill her?" by now tears were streaming from Tobias's eyes. "For the gold." "You disciple, greedy, selfish, money-hungry, man! Why would stay with her for twenty-one years and then kill her?"

"I was scared to do it. I hesitated every time. It was only until she told you of your inheritance that I knew it was now or never for me to take."

"So, you're telling me that everything that happened to me from that man trying to kidnap me to the house burning down in flames was you."

"Yes, it was me!"

Tobias didn't have words to express the rage boiling in his heart and soul. He grabbed his father once more, tackled him to the ground, and begun throwing punches into his face. "Enough!" Detective Greyson said, rushing over to the fight and grabbing Tobias by the shoulders.

Tobias shook his grasp off and continued beating his father with furious punches. He withdrew from his pocket a pocket knife which he had been holding around with him ever since he learned that someone had ill-wishes against him.

He took the knife and cut Bennett across the face. Bennett screamed in pain. Detective Greyson yanked Tobias off and took the knife from him. Tobias strained against his grip but eventually he calmed down and glared at his father. Bennett rose from the ground.

His face looked horrible. Blood trickled from the cut across. "This is not over" Tobias said, trying to catch his breath. "It is over. You will do nothing else" Greyson said. "Sure, I won't do anything more to my father who chose my mother for her wealth and killed her. I won't do anything more to him. Nothing at all."

"We have to go to the police department" Natasha said. "Get in the trap" Detective Greyson told Bennett and Torin. Detective Greyson sat at the top seat of the trap where the driver sits to control the horse. Tobias and Natasha sat in one row of seats in the trap while Bennett and Torin sat in the opposite seats.

Tobias heard the crack of the whip before the trap started along the bumpy road. Tobias glared at his father the whole way to the department. The trap pulled up at the department and the passengers descended it. Detective Greyson kept his gun in his hand as they walked the prisoners into the department.

"What's happening here?" a policeman walked up to them and asked. "Where's Mr. Dewey?" Detective Greyson asked. "Follow me" the policeman said. They took the stairs to the second floor and found Mr. Dewey's office room. The policeman knocked at the door. "Come in" Mr. Dewey said. He opened the door and walked in, followed by the rest. "How can I- Mr. Dewey froze at the sight of Torin and Bennett.

"We found the guilty suspects of the Pristine Hills Murder" Detective Greyson said. "How?" Mr. Dewey asked. "Tobias spotted them at the diner when he was with Natasha here, and she came to the house to tell me." "It was a rough pursuit but they arrived in time to stop them. You see the cut on Bennett's face? That's my work so you know."

"Why are you calling me by my name?" Bennett asked. "You know why" Tobias said. "And just how do you know these two are the killers?" Mr. Dewey asked. Detective Greyson pointed out the opposing facts in the polices' story. "You saw those facts, didn't you? You're not slow, Mr. Dewey."

"I didn't see those facts. I'm glad you pointed them out to me" Mr. Dewey said. "Yes you did. If Tobias saw them, you saw it also," Detective Greyson said. "We're bringing this case to court once more."

For the next week, Tobias attended the court trials. Every time he stepped foot into court and saw Bennett sitting up front with Torin and Mr. Dewey as guilty suspects, it didn't feel real. Tears would sting his eyes during the trial just to think that his father killed his mother. He found it hard to imagine that the person he thought loved and cared for him was actually the killer of his mother.

In one court trial, the guilty suspects were ordered to tell their part of the story behind Anne James murder.

24

CHAPTER 24

"At the time when I was supposed to be marrying Wendy Hudson, Anne James moved into Pristine Hills-

"You don't deserve to say her name" Tobias thought.

"She was a rich woman who wanted to build her own house in the neighborhood, so she employed construction workers to build her house. I was a construction worker at the time who was financially poor. Since I was good at my job however, the owner of the construction industry put me in charge of the project. Amongst us construction workers was Jack Oberon, who was a good friend of mines.

Because of I was in charge of the project, I was constantly interacting with Anne James. I learned that she was wealthy and she was investing half of her gold into the house. I admit that a desire for wealth was always in me, but I never thought it make do what I did. So, I acted as though I loved Anne and she loved me back but sincerely unlike I. Then two days before my wedding with Wendy, I told her that I changed my mind.

I admit that it was disgusting of me to give up true love for wealth. I loved Wendy, but my desire for wealth became stronger. Anne and I got married, settled into the house, and she bought a horse and trap so I could have a better job. Nothing in the house did I own. Two weeks after our marriage, she hired a lawyer and signed a will with me and Clara Ambrose as witnesses. The will said that her property will be the inheritance of her child when she had one.

I knew I had to do something to get that gold, but I didn't know where it was for she didn't tell anyone of the location. There were many times where I nearly planned to start my scheme, but some kind of fear and hesitance would stop me. I kept telling myself that I needed to create a plan and put it to action before it was too late.

Then Anne got pregnant with Tobias. We ended up raising him together until he turned twenty one. She told him of his inheritance. When I returned home that night and we were in bed, she told me that she told Tobias of his inheritance. I acted as if that was good, but inside I knew I had to act now if I wanted that gold. Tobias was growing and now he knew of his inheritance.

I stood up all night thinking of my plan. I didn't want to kill her myself, so I needed someone to hire. I thought of Torin Dewey, whom I met in a card club. We became friends and I learned that he was in need of money to pay off an important debt. So, I met him the following day and asked him if he would do anything to get that money to pay off his debt.

He said that his life depended on it and that he was up for anything. So, I explained my plan and purpose to him. He was surprised at what I was about to do, but he agreed to it anyway. I knew that Anne was leaving work at two pm and that time was nearing.

Torin positioned himself on the second floor of the abandoned building, where he had a clear view of the alleyway. When two pm hit and Anne exited the building, he shot her with an air gun. He had access to that kind of gun being that he was in the force.

Torin and I made sure to leave no clues of the killer, and to just allow the police to do their investigation and suspect whoever they suspected. And that's how it happened. I sent a letter to Torin to meet me in the woods so I could pay him for the job. The day after Anne was shot, we met in the woods during the afternoon. I paid Torin and asked him if he was willing to do one more job for me. He agreed to it. We were about to depart when Tobias surprised us by coming out from behind the tree.

At that moment, I couldn't be more thankful for the disguise I wore. Torin and I chose flight but Tobias pursued us. My scarf fell off during the pursuit. Tobias tripped over a log. He yelled at that us that he sweared by his flesh and bones that he would catch us and give us what he deserved.

The seriousness and anger in his voice and words shook me a bit, and when I arrived home, I knew I had to do something. So, I told Tobias at breakfast not to go to the woods because that's where kidnappers set up their traps. That is true. Everyone is aware of that.

I saw that it was Tobias's nature to be stubborn and independent because he attempted to argue with me. I didn't trust that he wouldn't return to the woods even after what I said, so I needed a better way to install fear into him. I told him another morning that a man had followed me, but that was false. When Tobias went out that day, I paid my friend Jack Oberon, who was still a poor construction worker at the industry a good amount if he followed Tobias on his way home.

That was what he did and Tobias obviously thought what I said was true. A few days after I paid Jack to attempt a fake kidnapping on Tobias when he went to the woods with his dog. But that went horribly wrong as Tobias managed to kill and returned home wounded.

After that plan went in a direction I didn't expect, I started asking myself if what I was doing was worth it.

Was the gold worth the headache and being constantly nervous about the police discovering the truth? I almost decided on giving myself in, but then I said, I didn't do all this for nothing. I wasn't going give up easily.

I needed to take the next step and that was learning where the gold was hidden in the house. So, I paid Torin to do the last job which he agreed to. That job was to pour gasoline around the house but leave the front door open. He lit a match and threw it on the gasoline before it blew up.

The household was aroused quickly by the strong fumes and soon everyone was in a state of panic. The women were ordered to evacuate while Tobias and I went to get the gold. That's when I learned that it was hidden in a safe behind the bookshelf in mines and Anne's bedroom, and the key was in the soil of a flower pot. I thought to myself, Anne was a clever woman.

When Tobias opened the safe, we both saw a black gemstone sitting atop the gold. It was an Opal gemstone. It was clear by the look on Tobias's face that Anne didn't tell him about it. I think she decided to leave him to discover it. At the sight of the priceless gem, my heart was racing with a desire to just snatch it. I knew then that what I was doing was going to be worth it in the end.

But when the house came down in ashes and Tobias had that outrageous attack infront of everyone, a sudden guilt overtook my heart. I begun regretting my actions and questioning them again. I found myself suddenly longing for Anne and realizing that during the time we were together, I had come to love her even if I faked it in the beginning. I realized that my desire for wealth just broke the beautiful family I had.

But there was no turning back or erasing my sins, so I decided the least I could do was stop everything but not give myself in. I made the decision that when the police close the case, I would flee Pristine Hills and perhaps travel to the other side of the world. And even though the gold was the reason I did all this, I would leave Tobias's inheritance for him because I didn't deserve it. It was his by right and he deserved it for everything I put him through.

Now if the police did recover the truth, I wouldn't attempt to flee. Prison was what I deserved anyways. I met with Torin to speak about the situation and pay him the rest of the money for the fire he created. There is where my story comes to an end."

25

●

CHAPTER 25

"Before I became a police officer, I was a bad and reckless teenager who spent most of my time on the streets. My father tried many times to advise me and guide me to a better path, because my ways was swallowing me into evil. But I always rejected my father's advise. He kept trying to guide me, but without my mother who died when I was four, he couldn't control a reckless teenager on his own.

I continued doing what I wanted, what pleased my desires till it eventually led to a disaster. I found myself caught up with a gang who committed crimes and made horrible deals with other gangs and even amongst themselves. As I grew into a young man, my mind started maturing and my eyes opened to the light. My father was heedless of what I was up to and the crimes I committed, but I wasn't going to tell him. He was the chief of the police department and I knew he couldn't afford to hide my secret.

That would jeopardize his life and title. He would lose his rank and everything he worked to build. I didn't want to be the cause of that. So, I decided now it was time for me to change because it was a good time. I spoke with the gang's leader. I explained to him that

I didn't want to be apart of the gang, but I promised and swore that I wouldn't give them away to the police.

The gang leader as well as the gang was easy going, and not one of those gangs where you can't leave or else they will hunt you down. But I had a deal with the leader from when I was in the gang, so he said that I needed to pay it off if I wanted to leave. He swore that if I fled without paying it off, he would hunt me down and kill me.

So, I started looking for ways to earn that large sum of money. I decided that a good way to earn it was to join the card club and win money by winning the matches. That's where I met Bennett James. We played cards together, won and lost matches, spoke with one another, and soon came to know enough where we became friends. We met occasionally at the club and played together.

He learnt of my payment and I learnt that he needed someone to do a job for him. Like that, we made a deal. I had the skills of a criminal and he had the money I needed. I couldn't believe how good things were for me. I did my job and he paid me.

Then there came the incident with Samuel Armando. When he was brought in, my father told Detective Jason Emery and Police officer Bob Martin that he needed time to think over what happened. I had already come up with a good story that fitted the facts and suspects we had.

Now, I needed to tell my father. So, when we went home, I told him the story. He pointed out the false factors within my story and said that the case wasn't finished yet. I desperately wanted it to be closed because all the time during this deal I had with Bennett James, I was afraid the police would discover the truth. I couldn't breathe even when knowing that the police were focused on Wendy Hudson, Ted Wilson, and Samuel and Dolores Armando.

So, I laid my situation plain to my father. I had my trust that he would hide it for me, being that I was his son and he loved me with more than his heart. It played out the way I expected. My father said we would use the story I came up with and state that Wendy Hudson, Ted Wilson, and Dolores Armando were the guilty suspects.

My story ends when I met Bennett James at the diner to retrieve the remainder of my payment."

26

EPILOGUE

"To your cells" the police officer said. He and several other officers walked the prisoners who wore orange suits to their cells. With them was Detective Greyson and Tobias. It pleased his heart to see his father in the orange prison attire.

This moment was like walking through a garden that was blossoming in flowers, but even better. The police locked Frank and Torin in a cell together and Bennett was in his own.

The police officer shoved Bennett into his cell and slammed the gate closed before twisting the key to lock it. The police officers and Detective Greyson started walking away, but Tobias walked up to the cell bars. He looked at his father with a pair of calm and collected eyes, but inside the flames of rage burned his heart and soul.

Bennett looked at Tobias in sympathy and guilt. "When we meet again in twenty years, it will be our last meeting" Tobias said. He fished out from the pocket of his coat a wedding ring box and opened it to expose the ring. Bennett recognized the ring to be Anne's wedding ring. The sympathy and guilt on his face vanished with the wind, replaced by fear. Tobias shot him a deadly glare, before returning the box to his pocket and walking away.

The last that Tobias heard from Pristine Hills was that Dolores got a divorce from Samuel at court. Samuel remained in prison for his illegal actions of helping immigrants across the border. Dolores moved on with her life and became engaged for marriage to Ted Wilson. It was a big deal when the neighborhood found out about Mr. Butcher's engagement.

Dwight Greyson became the head of the police force once Frank Dewey was removed from that position.

After the arrest of his father, Tobias disappeared without leaving a footprint behind. The police were unable to track him. When Natasha discovered a strip of paper that read "I love you", she and Dwight came to the conclusion that he left for good.

But nobody could be sure of the fate of Tobias James.